The Gammage Cup

Also by Carol Kendall
The Whisper of Glocken

The
GAMMAGE
CUP

A Novel of the Minnipins

Carol Kendall

Illustrated by Erik Blegvad

An Odyssey/Harcourt Young Classic
Harcourt, Inc.

Orlando   Austin   New York   San Diego   London

www.hmhco.com

First Harcourt Young Classics edition 2000
First Odyssey Classics edition 1990
First published 1959

Library of Congress Cataloging-in-Publication Data
Kendall, Carol, 1917–
The Gammage Cup: a novel of the Minnipins/ Carol Kendall;
illustrated by Erik Blegvad.
p. cm.
"An Odyssey/Harcourt Young Classic."
Spot illustrations.
Summary: A handful of Minnipins, a sober and sedate people,
rise up against the Periods, the leading family of an isolated mountain valley,
and are exiled to a mountain where they discover that the ancient enemies
of their people are preparing to attack.
[1. Fantasy.] I. Blegvad, Erik, ill. II. Title.
PZ7.K33Gam 2000
[Fic]—dc21 99-55279
ISBN 978-0-15-202487-1 ISBN 978-0-15-202493-2 (pb)

Printed in the United States of America

DOC 20 19 18

4500615753

To Paul

The Gammage Cup

1

In the long far off
Of the land Outside
Brave Minnipins lived
And some of them died.

Lost are their treasures, buried deep.

Till the Dry Time came
And the world was sand—
Then Minnipins fled
To a wetter land.

Lost are their treasures; in the
    ground they sleep.

And nobody knew
That the Minnipins went
To the land of the River,
Where they live content.

Lost are their treasures, and the
    secret they keep.

   —Gummy, *Scribbles*
    (Collected Works)

It was quite untrue that the Minnipins, or Small Ones, were a lost people, for *they* knew exactly where they were. They dwelt along the banks of the Watercress River in the Land Between the Mountains, where they fished and tended their famous watercress beds and grew their own peculiar reeds, which could be milled into flour or used for thatching or pulped into paper or woven into cloaks of mothwing softness.

It was a snug and secure valley, completely surrounded by unclimbable mountains, so perfectly made for stay-at-home, peace-loving Minnipins that it was no wonder they were to be found there. There were twelve villages in all, starting with Watersplash at the very head of the valley where the freshets foamed down the cliffs of old Snowdrift Mountain, and ending with Water Gap, where the waters of the river roared through the very heart of the craggy mountain known as Frostbite.

It was through this tunnel in Frostbite (according to legend) that the only remaining Minnipins on earth had traveled, under their leader Gammage, to reach the green valley in those old far-off days of the great Dry Time. The river was a mere muddy trickle then, like all the rivers of the land. It was said (by Walter the Earl, who made a study of such things from a few old moldy parchments in his possession) that the Minnipins were running for their lives from a savage band known as Mushrooms, or the Hairless Ones, when they entered the long tunnel, yanking their two-wheeled carts after them. They were only saved from being spitted and roasted for the Mushrooms' dinner by a miraculous rain, which filled the riverbed after they had come through the tunnel and washed out their pursuers. Once the river closed the underground passage, there was no way in or out of the Land Between the Mountains, except for high-flying birds—and Fooley the Balloonist, of course. But Fooley came along sometime later, and Fooley was special.

One of the twelve villages was Slipper-on-the-Water, which got its name (so the legend went on) when those first Minnipins paddled their rudely made boats up the Watercress to explore their new valley. It was at this spot that Gammage lost his left slipper overboard. For three days and three nights it floated on the water in the selfsame spot, never moving with the current. Clearly, this was a symbol not to be ignored. So it was that ten of the Minnipins never got to the head of the valley at all. They stayed at Slipper-on-the-Water, building their cottages of river clay and reed thatch, establishing their watercress beds, and raising their small families. But before Gammage and the others traveled on to found other villages along the Watercress, each of the ten drank deeply from the precious Cup of Wisdom that Gammage carried wrapped in silk and slung over his shoulder.

So much and no more was known of the far past, for no real records had been kept during the early ages. At least, none had ever been discovered, though Walter the Earl was convinced that they existed. His several fragments of ancient parchment hinted, he said (nobody else could decipher the old writing), of treasures buried in the village, possibly in his own garden. His cottage had the oldest foundation of any in Slipper-on-the-Water and was believed to have been the first meetinghouse in the village. So Walter the Earl dug up his garden and probed at the walls of his house in search of ancient scrolls and treasure, and occasionally buttonholed folk to talk about Historical Facts, while more sensible Minnipins worked at their practical jobs and, when they thought of Walter the Earl at all, considered him a dry old bore.

Now, in this year of Gammage 880, though Slipper-on-the-Water had the usual river-clay cottages with reed thatch, lived in by the usual Minnipins and Minnipin children, it was by no means an ordinary village.

For one thing, there were those few villagers

known as the Periods. Periods were special—everyone agreed to that. Not only did they have a special way of spelling their names, but they wore a special air of dignity, and, of course, they held most of the village offices. It had been this way in Slipper-on-the-Water ever since the time of Fooley the Balloonist, for the Periods were the descendants of Fooley, and that explained everything as far as the villagers were concerned.

It was just four hundred and forty years ago that Fooley, afterward known as Fooley the Magnificent or The Great Fooley, had sailed away over the cliffs of Snowdrift in a balloon of reed silk and woven willow, the first, last, and only balloon ever constructed in the Land Between the Mountains. Even more miraculous to ground-loving Minnipins, he had sailed back just one hundred and twenty-nine days later, bringing with him a case full of curiosities from the Land Beyond the Mountains. But as though to underline the moral that Minnipins were meant to stay at home, the balloon contraption had burst when he landed, scattering its contents, including Fooley, over several Minnipin acres of ground. When Fooley was picked up, he had no recollection of what he had seen in the Land Beyond the Mountains. If it hadn't been for the curiosities and the queer book he had filled with notes, Fooley would in time have become a misty legend, and Slipper-on-the-Water only number ten of the twelve very ordinary Minnipin villages spread along the banks of the Watercress.

But as it was, the Periods, descendants of that long-ago adventurer, were special. Though Minnipins in general never strayed far from their homes (always excepting the mayors of the villages, who once a year made the long trip to Watersplash for the Big Meeting), the fame of these descendants had gone up and down the valley. Periods were like that.

But it wasn't only the Periods who made Slipper-on-the-Water different. There were three Minnipins in the village who were usually referred to by their neighbors as "Oh, Them." "They" were not considered respectable; They were a law among themselves; They lived alone instead of marrying and raising families, as normal Minnipins did; worst of all, They flaunted cloaks of such an outlandish hue that it was shaming to be seen talking to them. Furthermore, the "Oh, Thems" didn't properly work at anything: Walter the Earl spent his time digging holes in the ground in his ridiculous search for hidden treasure; Curley Green was usually to be seen sitting on her stool in a corner of the marketplace, blobbing pictures onto stretched reed paper, and Gummy—well, Gummy was bone-idle.

Gummy was never seen doing anything but wearing a dreamy look along with his sun-colored cloak and peaked hat. He disappeared for hours at a time in his tiny boat, but where he went and what he did nobody knew, though there were rumors aplenty. Only two things were surely known about Gummy: he was overfond of childish pranks, and he made rhymes. Not proper poems, such as the one brought back by Fooley, now hanging in the museum, but scribbles—nonsense rhymes about rain and birds and flowers and the wind, and they bubbled out of him as water bubbles from a spring.

Then, of course, there was Muggles. Muggles couldn't be called one of "Them," exactly, but she wasn't just an ordinary villager, either. While it was true that she dutifully wore the Minnipin green cloak and brown-weave dress, it cannot be denied that upon occasion she tied up her middle with a vivid orange sash.

Besides being the caretaker of the Fooley curiosities in the museum, she was a candymaker, which was a good steady sort of thing to be, but on the other hand she distressed the tidy Minnipin housewives by keeping her house in a deplorable muddle. She was a collector of odds and ends and bits and pieces (another good trait), but they overflowed her tiny cottage until it was next to impossible

to step inside, and that was disgraceful. There had been complaints, of course, and only last year the mayor himself had begged her to tidy up, like a good Minnipin. Ever anxious to please, Muggles had tried hard, but the more she put away, the less able was she to find anything. Gradually, the articles she had neatly folded into cupboards slipped back into their old places on the floor, closets disgorged their precise piles of oddments, and drawers leaked their contents, until once more Muggles knew exactly where everything was.

So Muggles was something of a trial to Slipper-on-the-Water, but it was agreed that there was no real harm in her. She was always ready to oblige, always in a good humor, and if she was a little simpleminded, why, she could hardly be blamed for that. Being simpleminded never interfered with her candy recipes or the job she had been given at the museum.

The museum! Muggles awoke with the panicky feeling that she had overslept. She shot out of bed like a surfacing trout and then stood blinking in the chill half-light of her little room. *How very odd*, she thought in her sleep-fogged mind. *How very odd that it is still so dark. What can have happened to the sun?* Groping her way to the window, which overlooked the marketplace, she peered anxiously through the slatted reed shade. There had been rain during the night, for the cobblestones gleamed wet in the dim flare of the reed-light still burning fitfully in the center of the marketplace. But why was the sun so late in appearing, today of all days, when the mayor was coming home from the Big Meeting? Still convinced that she had overslept, Muggles stood winking and blinking at the deserted cobblestones. Where had everybody got to? Why wasn't the square full of green-cloaked figures hustling and bustling about to make ready for the mayor's return?

Then with a sigh of relief she saw a line of golden fire on top of the Sunset Mountains in the west. Why, the sun must be just rising—only there was something wrong about that, too, wasn't there? Suddenly she heard the pat-pat of soft woven slippers on the cobblestones of the square. Rubbing her blurred eyes, she made out the figure of Gummy, one of Them. He was coming from the Street Going to the River, and stumbling across the marketplace as though he had just got off a dizzy-swing at the fun fair. His yellow cloak drooped from his shoulders, and his peaked hat looked wilted. In the middle of the marketplace he stopped and stared up at the orange fire on the mountains for several moments before he staggered on. Muggles watched him going toward his own shabby cottage. Then he stopped again and veered to the right. A moment later he had gone into Walter the Earl's house.

Muggles blinked and stared and blinked again. Odder and odder. The reed-light continued to flicker, casting its weird shadows over the cottages around the square and the four public buildings in the center.

The door through which Gummy had gone opened once more, and he came out, this time accompanied by Walter the Earl, his gold-embroidered cloak slung around his shoulders. They both looked up at the Sunset Mountains—but now the fire had disappeared! While Muggles was pondering this further oddity, Gummy and Walter the Earl moved back toward Walter the Earl's house where they spent some minutes inspecting the mounds of earth in the garden. Finally, Gummy trudged off to his cottage, and Walter the Earl picked up a spade and plunged it into the ground in a spot close up to the house itself. And still the reed-light flickered eerily over the wet cobblestones of the empty marketplace . . .

Muggles stumbled back to her bed, struggling to make sense out of this very queer morning. It was not until her feet grew toasty warm under the comforter that the explanation occurred to her. *What a ninny I am*, she thought with a drowsy laugh. *It's not the sun that's late, it's me that's early. I was having a dream. I might have known when I saw the sun rising in the west that it was a dream. But what a queer dream to have, and it seemed so real.*

Yawning mightily, she snuggled deeper into her feather bed and let sleep creep back into her body.

Meanwhile, the sun rose quite properly from behind the Sunrise Mountains in the east, dispelling the light mist in the valley. The lamplighter extinguished the reed-light, sniffing hungrily at the yeasty aroma from Loaf the Baker's ovens, and the village stirred into life.

When the sun's rays finally touched Muggles's face, her eyes snapped open like window blinds suddenly released. She *had* overslept! There had been a sort of dream about oversleeping, she remembered fuzzily, and now she had *really* done it. Biting off a yawn, she floundered out of the jumble of comforters and pillows, and began reaching here and there for her clothes, which she always left, for convenience's sake, on the floor. There was no time for a bath, which was just as well, since her little bathing tub was full of odds and ends that had not yet found their way to a permanent keeping-place.

"A place for everything, and the more things in the place the better," Muggles murmured to herself, for there was nobody else to talk to. She paused in her dressing operations to cast a sharp glance around the room, just to reassure herself that nothing had leaped out of one pile into another during the night. But all was in perfect order, neat and tidy, the way she liked it—the far-corner pile, the hearthstone pile, the under-the-table pile. . . .

Muggles came to with a start. *Idle dreamers have nothing to put in the pot*, she told herself sharply. But she had a curious feeling that today was different from other days, that the very air she breathed was full of a strange excitement, that something not altogether pleasant was about to happen.

"Nonsense," she scoffed, reaching for her slipper. "There'll be a strange excitement not altogether pleasant indeed if I don't get over to that museum pretty soon. And the mayor coming home and all!" She slipped her fat little feet into her slippers and gave the points on the toes a jerk to make them stand upright. "It's what comes of dreaming silly dreams about suns coming up in the west where they've no right to be, that's all. Next I'll be dreaming there are real fires on the Sunset Mountains, and *then* where'll we all be?"

She struggled into her brown-weave dress and looked around for her brown sash, but it had somehow lost itself. No matter—today was a special day, with the mayor coming home from Watersplash. It was a day for a cheerful sash. She plunged her hand into the corner cupboard and unearthed the orange streamer that she saved for big events. Putting it around her middle, she tied it tightly, letting the ends tumble down the front.

There was no time for breakfast, so she delved into the far-corner pile, down past a box containing five magic pebbles, the pot of new healing ointment concocted from fifteen herbs and willow bark, a packet of glitter-stones, the length of orange cloth she had dyed herself, a jar of poppy seeds, a green hat with a hole in the top, one mitten for the left hand, and two ribbons, to a little woven-reed basket, from which she extracted one of the five packets of pepmints. Then, throwing her green cloak about her shoulders, she opened the door and stepped out into the sunshine and bustle of the marketplace.

The cobblestoned square looked newly washed from the night's rain. Muggles frowned in sudden remembrance of her dream, and then shook her head impatiently. Today Minnipins of all ages were scurrying about the marketplace, green cloaks flying in the breeze. Round rosy housewives, their brown-weave dresses tucked up, were scrubbing their doorstones or polishing the silver doorknobs on their watercress-green doors, while children were watering the flowers that grew around the family trees.

Down the Street Going to the River, Muggles could see the town clerk's bald head shining as he strung up welcoming garlands over the dock, while Mingy the Money Keeper stood at the bottom of the ladder and glared at him. The lines of one of Gummy's scribbles, which the children had got hold of and liked to chant, ran through Muggles's head.

> Oh, Mingy was stingy,
> So everyone said,
> With gold in his closet
> And under his bed.
> Oh, Mingy was stingy,
> Or so I've been told.
> He never did aught
> But count out his gold.
> Oh, Mingy was stingy,
> 'Tis said oft enough.
> I'd say it myself,
> Believed I that stuff.

She was immediately ashamed of herself, but Gummy's scribbles had a way of jingling round in one's head.

It was then that Muggles did the first of many strange things. Late as she was, she turned and started back around the marketplace instead of crossing directly to the museum. *I'm being foolish*, she scolded herself, but she kept right on going.

She slowed as she passed Gummy's shabby cottage, but there was no sign of him. Well, what had she expected? And if she had seen him, what then? She could hardly stop and ask him if he by any chance remembered being in her dream! The doorknob on his scuffed door needed polishing, Muggles noted with disapproval, and then remembered that she had forgotten to polish her own that morning.

Neither was Curley Green to be seen. Muggles came to a full stop to gaze at the door, which was as scarlet as Curley Green's cloak and blazed in the morning sunlight like a bright welcoming smile. What would it be like to live behind a door like that! Not that Muggles ever *would*, she assured herself quickly—green was the only proper color for doors—but all the same, it would be exciting to be invited through that scarlet door someday. It was rumored in the village that not only did Curley Green refuse to paint real paintings such as that brought back by Fooley, but that she actually blobbed pictures on the walls of her house! Of course, it was probably just gossip, but all the same . . .

The scarlet door suddenly swung open, and Muggles found herself smiling directly into Curley

Green's blue eyes that always seemed to be faintly mocking. She gave a little gasp and began to move on.

"Good morning, Muggles," Curley Green called. "Were you looking for me?" Her scarlet cloak was flung carelessly over her sky-blue dress, and her light silky hair blew about her face like milkweed fluttering in a breeze. Under one arm she carried the box of paints that always went with her.

Muggles paused uncertainly. "G-good morning. I was just—won't you—would you like a pepmint?"

"Thank you." Curley Green transferred her paintbox to her other hand and dipped into the crumpled bag that Muggles proffered. Muggles helped herself from the bag, and they both stood there, solemnly sucking on the creamy bits and looking shyly at each other.

Why, she looks nice, Muggles thought with surprise. *Sort of—well, as though you could tell her things.*

"I was looking at your door," Muggles burst out. "I hope you don't mind. It—that is, your door— well, it sort of *smiled* at me." She stopped in confusion. It was saying just this kind of thing that made people laugh at her. She looked timidly at Curley Green. "I don't expect that makes good sense, a door smiling, does it?"

"Why ever not?" Curley Green said. "Have you ever noticed how the mayor's door frowns?"

Muggles laughed a little nervously, for nobody ever made jokes about anybody as important as the mayor, who was a Period. "Have—have another pepmint, do," she urged.

They moved off toward the museum, crossing the Small Road Going Nowhere. Muggles paused to look, not at the scurrying figures along the road, but at the distant Sunset Mountains, hazed in a smoky mist.

"I wonder what they're really like, the mountains," she said, remembering her strange dream. She would have liked to tell Curley Green about the fiery light on the mountains, but dreams lost their wonder when you told them. You had to keep on saying, "Well, I can't describe just the way it was, but . . ." or "Well, then suddenly I wasn't in the same place at all, only I can't explain how I got somewhere else . . ." No, dreams were not for telling.

Curley Green shifted her paintbox to the other arm. "Gummy says they are full of old gold mines. Like a honeycomb, almost. And there's a waterfall that dashes down—that's where the Little Trickle comes from. And the top of the cliff is so high and so straight that you think it will fall over on you when you look up."

"Gold mines!"

"That's right," Curley Green said matter-of-factly. "Silver, too, probably. Walter the Earl says Minnipins used to be great miners. Someday he is going with Gummy to see the old mines." She stared off into the distance where a bluish haze capped the crags of the Sunset Mountains. "I think perhaps I should like to go with them," she added slowly.

Muggles pressed a hand to her forehead to still the whirling motion inside. To talk so calmly about going into the wilds beyond the safety of the village, out of sight of houses and green cloaks and the old familiar cobblestones of the marketplace! Gold and silver mines! What was a mine like? And how did Gummy know so much about the mountains? She turned suddenly to Curley Green as a fearful thought struck her.

"You don't mean—has . . . has Gummy *been* there?" she asked in a hushed whisper.

Curley Green's blue eyes mocked her. "Of course. How else would he know about the mines?"

I really should be at the museum, Muggles thought in a panic. *I shouldn't be mixing myself up with Them. Gold and silver mines. Waterfalls. Cliffs that might fall down. Digging holes to find old treasures.*

She caught hold of Curley Green's free hand. "Oh, please don't even think of going," she begged. "Terrible things might happen. You mustn't ever go off from the village. It's not safe at all, you know!"

"But Gummy goes," said Curley Green with great calm. "He's built himself a house on the Little Trickle, up near the mountains."

A house! "Whatever for?" asked Muggles. "He's *got* a house, right here where a house should be."

Curley Green just looked at her. "Well, now he has two houses. The other one is made of stone, he says, and it has a front door and a back door, though I suspect the reason for that is he got tired of carrying stones and found it easier to make an extra door. Someday he's promised to take me there." She turned to gaze again at the Sunset Mountains. "You could go, too, if you liked," she added.

"Oh no, I couldn't—I wouldn't!" cried Muggles, shrinking away. "And I really must be off now—the museum—the mayor's homecoming . . . It's—it's been nice talking to you, but . . . Some other time . . ." and she began to hurry on across the road, past Walter the Earl's cottage with its unsightly mounds all around it. Even as she passed, a shovelful of dirt landed on top of the newest mound and sprinkled down its sides. *Digging holes produces nothing but holes*, Muggles thought severely, and hurried a little faster. Behind her the unseen Walter the Earl plopped another shovelful of dirt on the heap.

The museum was one of the four public buildings in the marketplace. Like any proper Minnipin building, it was made of white-painted clay and thatched with reed, and of course it had a watercress-green door. But over that door, so that nobody could mistake it for a mere cottage, was lettered in the official village painter's neatest script:

Fooley Museum

In the second corner was a building just like it except that the script read, this time:

Fooley Hall
Meeting House

The third building, exactly like the other two, said:

House of the Mayor

And the fourth building was labeled:

Supplys

The official village painter sometimes made errors in spelling, but since he was a descendant of Fooley the Magnificent, nobody liked to call attention to his mistakes, and "Supplys" the general store remained.

Muggles reached the museum and pushed open the watercress-green door. Only then did she look back to where she had left Curley Green, but Curley Green appeared to have forgotten all about her. She was standing on top of the fresh pile of dirt, talking to Walter the Earl. Or rather, he was talking, and pointing in the direction of the Sunset Mountains. Then he took up his spade and slid down the mound out of sight, but Curley Green still stood there, gazing into the distance. With a shiver of apprehension, Muggles slipped into the peaceful silence of the museum. There were lots of reasons why Walter the Earl might be pointing to the mountains, she told herself. It had nothing to do with her dream. . . . She went quickly around the four walls, opening lattice blinds and letting the air in through the windows.

A bar of sunlight fell across the Gammage Slipper on the pedestal in the middle of the room. It showed a thin film of dust on the ancient brown leather. Clicking her tongue against the roof of her mouth, Muggles hurried over and blew vigorously.

Dust motes danced in the air, then slowly began to settle once more. With a guilty look behind her, Muggles lifted the precious slipper off its green cushion and rubbed it with one end of her orange sash. The Gammage Slipper was the most venerated object in the Land Between the Mountains—always excepting the Gammage Cup, of course, but that was kept at Watersplash where Gammage had carried it eight hundred eighty years ago, and though folk all up and down the Watercress River yearned to drink of its wisdom, at Watersplash the cup remained. Even the mayor of Slipper-on-the-Water, with his persuasive ways, had failed to convince the Council of Twelve Mayors that the Gammage Cup belonged in Slipper-on-the-Water where there was a museum to house it properly.

Reverently replacing the slipper on its green cushion, Muggles next looked to Fooley's Balloon, although there was not much of it left to arrange. The woven willow basket had been mended and remended by Crambo the Basketmaker and Crambo's father and grandfather before him, but the strong reed-silk that had once ballooned over Fooley's head was tattered with age. Muggles dusted it by the simple expedient of blowing on it as hard as she could. Then she turned to the table that held Fooley's Book.

This tindery volume she opened with careful fingers to the page which the mayor liked best. (He was the most direct descendant of Fooley the Magnificent, being the eldest son of the eldest son of the oldest son, and so on back to the eldest son of Fooley himself.) The page held a list of strange words neatly printed in Fooley's hand. Until the day of his death, Fooley could never remember what the words meant, but his wife was sure they were the names of friends he had made in the Land Beyond the Mountains. Very distinguished and special-looking the names were, too, all with periods after them.

Ltd.
Co.
Bros.
Wm.
Geo.
Eng.
Scot.
Etc.
Rd.
St.
Ave.
&.

So Fooley's wife proceeded to have a batch of

children (instead of the usual two to a family) and to each child she gave one of the distinguished names, including the period, of course. Nobody could ever mistake a descendant of Fooley the Magnificent for an ordinary Minnipin. Some of the ordinary Minnipins, who were perhaps envious, said you could not only never mistake them—you couldn't even pronounce them. Fooley's wife retorted that it only took a bit of imagination. She got Fooley, when he was an old, old man sitting idle in the sun, to print out a second list beside the first.

Muggles carefully wiped the dust off the book with her orange sash, and then, as she did every morning, read down the two lists:

Ltd.	Litted (to rhyme with fitted)
Co.	Coe
Bros.	Bross
Wm.	Wim
Geo.	Gee-oh
Eng.	Eng
Scot.	Scot
Etc.	Etcuh
Rd.	Rid
St.	Stuh
Ave.	Ave (to rhyme with save)
&.	????

Since Fooley's day, the names had been used over and over again, for his grandchildren, his great-grandchildren, and *their* great-grandchildren, but none of them was ever called "&." because nobody, not even Fooley's wife, could think how to pronounce it.

It must be grand, Muggles often thought, to have one of those names and see it written there in the book. But today there was no time for idle vaporings. She marched across the room to set the painting straight. It always went crooked when the door opened or shut.

The Painting   The Family Tree

Of all the curiosities that had been pitched out of Fooley's balloon, the painting was the only one to fall into the Watercress River. When it had been fished out, nobody knew what it was, but fortunately Fooley had listed in his book the names of the curiosities, and when everything else was checked off—like the family tree, the poem, the hourglass—it was obvious that the remaining item was a painting. The bath in the Watercress had done it no good. Though the colors of the squares, triangles, circles, and shields were clear enough, and the interconnecting black lines intact, the piece of parchment looked as though inky fingers had daubed it. But daubs or no daubs, the Periods (and therefore the ordinary villagers) adopted the painting for their own. Ever since Fooley's time, a painting was a pattern of colored shapes connected by black lines, following the classical example. Had it not been for the children—and Curley Green—who persisted in making pictures of scenes or things or people instead of precise patterns, the older art would have been lost entirely.

Muggles had long ago given up trying to understand the painting—that was for the clever Periods—so after flicking it with the ends of her sash, she moved on to the family tree hanging on the same wall. It was strange to think that before Fooley made his balloon voyage there wasn't a tree in the whole village. Trees were for forests, not villages, just as houses were for villages, not forests.

But when Fooley returned with the picture of a great willow growing in front of a house, the idea of a family tree in every garden had taken firm root with the Minnipins. Such was the planting fever in Fooley's time that today there wasn't a cottage in Slipper-on-the-Water without a fine willow growing in front of it.

"And a fine willow is a fine thing," Muggles murmured to herself. "There's nothing like willow for an ailment, whether it's a cut hand or a stomach-ache or bad dreams . . ."

Bad dreams . . . Her dream of the morning, which had been crouching at the back of her head, leaped suddenly sharp and clear into her mind—the line of orange fire on the mountains . . . Gummy pointing to it . . . Walter the Earl plunging his spade into the ground . . .

But Walter the Earl really *had* plunged his spade into the ground—in the selfsame spot she had seen in her dream, for there it was that the new hole was dug. And he, too, had pointed to the mountains to show Curley Green. . . . Show her what?

Nonsense, she scoffed, and gave the family tree an angry flick of her sash. *It's that Gummy's fault. Folks stay decently home in their beds and other folk wouldn't dream about them.*

Then she stood quite still. What if . . . just

supposing . . . of course it wasn't possible . . . but . . .

What if it hadn't been a dream?

What if the light she had seen this morning had been fires on the mountains? But that was more nonsense. How *could* there be fires on the Sunset Mountains?

Scarcely aware of what she was doing, Muggles walked out the door of the museum and across the cobblestones to Walter the Earl's house. Curley Green was sitting with her back to the willow tree, facing the cottage. Against her drawn-up knees she held a big strip of birch bark, which she was dabbing with her paintbrush. But the blob she was painting was not the scene before her—the white clay cottage with its green door, the mound of fresh earth beside it. She was painting instead—but Muggles had only the briefest glimpse of the blob before Curley Green, hearing her step, flipped it over and held it suspended between her fingers.

What Muggles *thought* she saw was—her dream! Surely that had been the marketplace, wet and glistening in the expiring flicker of the reed-light; Gummy lurching across the cobblestones; and high above the village in the black distance, tongues of orange flame licking the top of the Sunset Mountains.

"You've come back," said Curley Green.

"Yes, I—I wanted to talk to Walter the Earl."

"He's not very talkative this morning." With great care Curley Green propped the birch bark against the trunk of the willow, with the picture facing in.

Muggles swallowed the dryness out of her throat. "The—that picture . . . Could I see it?"

Curley Green jerked her head up. But just then they heard a clanking, huffing, scrambling sound that made them both swing around to look at the dirt heap. There was a muffled exclamation, and a moment later a toiling figure emerged from the pit beyond the mound, hauling an iron box behind him.

It was Walter the Earl. Dirt encrusted his thick eyebrows, and rivulets of perspiration streaked his long stern nose. He stood commandingly on top of the mound, straddling the iron box, and blinked into the bright sunlight. Then, seeing Curley Green and Muggles below him, he smiled a slow triumphant smile. He raised a solemn hand, and his voice rang in the sunlit morning.

"I have found the ancient treasures!"

2

From out of the Then
And into the Now,
From the There to the Here
Come the Why and the How.

—Gummy, *Scribbles*
(Collected Works)

The ancient treasures! Muggles felt the blood pound into her head.

Curley Green glanced swiftly about the market-place, but no one was looking their way. "Better get that out of sight," she warned. "There are noses in the village sharp as needles, and if you don't want it taken away from you before you've even looked at it—"

"And this isn't all," Walter the Earl was going on. "There are boxes and boxes—" He stopped abruptly. "You're right, Curley Green. Not a word must be said." He frowned down at Muggles. "What about *her*?"

Curley Green hesitated and then, her eyes on Muggles's orange sash, said, "She's all right. Aren't you, Muggles?"

Muggles stared numbly from one to the other. "I'm—I'm all right," she said in a husky whisper, hardly aware that she was committing herself to anything.

"Come and see for yourselves." Walter the Earl beckoned them to follow and, taking hold of the iron box, slid from sight down into the pit.

Clambering to the top of the mound behind Curley Green, Muggles gazed into the hole with astonishment. It went deep, deep as a room is high, but the most surprising thing about it was the solid wall of stones which it exposed—foundation stones far beneath the cottage! At the bottom of the pit were pieces of rock which Walter the Earl had chipped out of the wall just above, making an opening large enough to crawl through.

"In here," came Walter the Earl's hollow voice from the opening.

They skidded down into the hole, and Curley Green slipped through the aperture with ease, but Muggles almost got stuck and had to wriggle herself free. She emerged into a dim chill stone chamber lighted by a single candle, which Walter the Earl had stuck on the floor. Iron boxes lined the walls to the wooden ceiling; iron boxes were stacked in the center of the floor; iron boxes were everywhere the eye looked.

"But what is *in* them?" asked Curley Green. "Are they *really* the treasure?"

Walter the Earl tapped the small chest he had dragged with him. "This contains ancient scrolls. As for the rest, we'll have to see." He pushed at the lid of the iron box nearest him. It didn't move. Snatching up a bar of iron lying on the floor, he pried at the lid. With a screak and a groan, it slowly opened. Curley Green snatched up the candle and with Muggles leaned over to see the contents of the chest.

"But it's just old black pieces of iron!" Muggles cried in dismay.

Walter the Earl reached in and picked up one of the objects.

"A knife!" exclaimed Curley Green. "But what a big one! Why would anybody want such a big knife?"

Walter the Earl thoughtfully ran his finger down the flat of the long blade. It was ugly and black and heavy, set in a plain haft that fitted snugly in his hand. He held the long knife out at arm's length and made a sudden slash with it. Muggles shrieked and jumped back.

"It's a wicked thing!" she cried.

"And so it should be—for killing wicked enemies." Walter the Earl drew his brows together in concentration. "But somehow I am disappointed. I thought it would have more beauty. And the edge seems dull."

"Oh, do put it away," Muggles pleaded. "We're not enemies. There aren't any enemies in the Land Between the Mountains. Put it away, Walter the Earl, before somebody is hurt." And she wrung her hands.

"That's what folk have been repeating for a great many years," said Walter the Earl absently. "And so they regard it as fact." He gave a snort of disgust. "Fact! What do they know about fact! However"— he looked fondly at the ugly black blade, and his voice became brisk—"it wants cleaning. Can you make me one of your polishes, my good Muggles? I must set to work to clean this—this knife."

Curley Green tugged impatiently at the lid of another box. "What do you suppose is in the rest of these?"

"Easily discovered," said Walter the Earl. He inserted the end of his crowbar beneath the lid and pried up the top. As the light of the candle glinted on the contents, Muggles gasped and fell back.

"Bodies! Oh, close the lid, quick. This is a horrible thing you have found!"

But Walter the Earl lifted out the topmost object, a terrible metallic head with a snout and enormous blue and gold plumes blossoming at the top. Even as he handled it, the snout clinked open as though the head would speak, and Walter the Earl all but dropped it in fright.

Curley Green shook so that the candle almost went out. "Is it—what is it? Oh, don't put it on—it may be magic!"

She was too late. Walter the Earl slipped the horrible hollow mask over his own head.

"Take it off!" Muggles cried, retreating toward the opening. "Take it off before—"

Curley Green began to laugh—a shaky little laugh, but heartening in the flickering gloom of the damp vault. "You look like a fish!"

Walter the Earl put his hands up to the snout of the helmet and pushed it up on his forehead. "Hand me some of those other pieces in the chest. I think I know what they are for!"

Curley Green gingerly plucked a clanking metal leg from the box, then another, and laid them on the floor. To the heap she added two jointed arms and finally a body piece. When she and Muggles had helped Walter the Earl into the surprisingly light metal garments, he was transformed into a terrible creature, but when he moved, he squeaked in all directions.

Muggles clapped her hands to her ears. "You need oiling!"

Walter the Earl nodded with satisfaction. "And polishing. You can see that it will be bright as the sun once it's cleaned." He cast another puzzled look at the long dull black knife. "Queer," he murmured.

They set to work more quickly, shifting boxes about and prying open the lids. There were more of the knives and the metal bodies; there were scarlet-and-gold banners; there were large flat pieces of metal with wrist straps in the middle; and then Muggles threw back the top of a chest whose contents glittered and flashed. Cloaks! But more splendid cloaks than any she could have imagined! With trembling fingers she took one out and held it up for the others to see. Woven of gold thread and encrusted with twinkling red and green and white stones, it was a cascade of colored fire in the dark vault.

Muggles caught her breath. "But do you think anybody ever *wore* these? They're not—they don't *look* like Minnipin cloaks! Ordinary ones, that is," she added quickly with a sidelong glance at the others.

Walter the Earl took the cloak from her and put its stiff crackling folds about his shoulders. A second and third he drew from the box and draped about Muggles and Curley Green. Then he snatched up the long black knife and waved it in an arc above his head. "Advance the host!" he cried. "Death to the enemy!"

Muggles gave a shudder. "I wish you wouldn't do things like that."

"The mayor won't like this," Curley Green said.

"Ltd. doesn't like anything that happened before Fooley," replied Walter the Earl. "The mayor has river water running in his veins instead of blood. Tell me this," and he scowled fiercely at them from under the visor of his helmet. "Has it ever occurred to you that if Fooley could leave this valley in a balloon, then it is possible for enemies to enter the valley in the same way?"

"But—but Fooley was different," Muggles stammered, frightened again. "Nobody else knows how to make a balloon, do they?"

"How do you know what folk do or do not do outside the Land Between the Mountains? What facts do you have on the subject?" retorted Walter the

Earl. "How do you know that a great force is not assembled this very minute to descend on us as though we were fish in Fin's fishing tank at the fair?"

Muggles could feel her legs begin to tremble. The fires on the mountain! "I—that's what I—"

"You're frightening Muggles," Curley Green said. She was rummaging in a box that contained strange long golden tubes ending in flaring edges, like trumpet flowers. Puzzled, she examined a trumpet flower, and then tilted the tube to look at the other end. Was one supposed to blow into it?

"It is time somebody in this sleepy valley was frightened," Walter the Earl began fiercely, just as Curley Green put the golden tube to her mouth and blew with all her might. The fearful blast exploded against the four walls. Muggles shrieked, and Walter the Earl staggered back, fell over a box, and landed on the floor in a din of clanking, squeaking metal. "Wh-what was that?" he stammered.

"I don't know." Curley Green held the golden tube toward him. "It looked as though it should be blown into, so I blew. Do you want to try?"

"No, no," Muggles begged, her hands over her ears. "You'll bring everybody in the village running to see."

Walter the Earl nodded approvingly as he took

the golden tube into his hands. "I wonder . . ." he mused. "Is it some sort of music pipe?"

"Music!" Muggles said with a snort. "Nobody could hear it without running all the way to the Sunset Mountains!"

"Aha! You have hit upon it, my good Muggles. This, then, is something to frighten the enemy." He looked at her with respect.

Muggles felt herself going pink with pleasure. "Perhaps," she said hopefully, "perhaps the ancient scrolls will tell us all about these things—the trumpet flower and the long knives and the metal suits and everything."

"Excellent thought!" Walter the Earl exclaimed. Then he looked around blankly. "But where *is* the little box?"

"You're leaning against it," said Curley Green.

"So I am." Walter the Earl swiveled awkwardly in his metal suit to get at the small chest. "More light, if you please, my dear Curley Green."

She brought the candle closer, and the three of them bent over the chest. Walter the Earl threw back the lid. Scroll upon scroll lay inside, yellow with age, their ribbons faded. Reverently, he picked up the top scroll and untied the ribbon. The parchment crackled as he unrolled it and held it under the light. Muggles stared blankly at the queer squiggles that filled the page, but Walter the Earl nodded.

"It's the old writing," he said. "Like the fragments that have been handed down through my family."

"Yes, yes," Curley Green said hastily, for everybody knew all about that ancient settler who had written an account of how the Minnipins had fled from the Mushrooms through the tunnel into the Land Between the Mountains. "But do read this to us."

"Hmm. Yes." Walter the Earl wrinkled up his forehead and bent his stern nose to the task. " 'Be it known,' hmm, er . . . 'that this . . . that this. . . .' Hmm . . . yes . . . it is a very difficult hand to read, but I think . . . ah, yes, here we are:

" 'Be it known that this chest of scrolls and all the other chests of armor, swords, shields, trumpets, battle flags, and war cloaks which were brought to the Land Between the Mountains by that great leader Gammage, and left in the care of one of my forebears, were sealed into this vault of the Old Meetinghouse by Walter, the Seventeenth Earl, in the year of Gammage 480, there to rest until somebody is once again interested in the glorious history of the Minnipins.

" 'It is forty years since the Fool returned from his balloon ride. Old ways are forgotten. The practice of arms is forbidden. Minnipins have grown soft and foolish and dangerously complacent. Even the Sacred Secret of the Swords is scoffed at as an elvan tale not to be believed.

" 'Be it noted that I dutifully offered the contents of these chests to the new mayor Ltd. for the museum now a-building, but his reply was that nobody is interested in the dead past. Lest these precious relics fall into disrespectful hands, I enclose them in this underground vault with the exception of a few fragments of parchment. They give a hint of the treasures contained herein, and I leave them in the possession of my eldest son's family, in hopes that at some distant time another Walter the Earl, untainted by the Fool's blood, will love the old ways enough to read the fragments and search until he unearths these treasures.

" 'It is my belief that such a one will appear when he is needed for the safety of his people. Let him believe in the swords and teach others to believe in their secret before it is too late.

" 'Signed by his hand,
" 'Walter, the Seventeenth Earl,
sometimes known as Walter the Obtuse' "

There was silence in the dim vault except for the crackle of the parchment in Walter the Earl's hands and the sputter of the candle.

" 'The Sacred Secret of the Swords,' " Curley Green said at last. "What can it mean? And what *are* swords?"

Walter the Earl shook his head. "It is a lost word. But I wonder . . ." He picked up the long black knife and examined it, turning it over and over in his hands. "I feel that the answer lies here," he said with a frown. "Sword . . . sword . . ." Over and over he turned it, seeking out its secret. But the blade remained dull and heavy in his hand.

"Trumpet," said Muggles suddenly. "That's what the horrid noise is—a trumpet. Because it looks like a trumpet flower."

"Yes, oh yes," said Curley Green. "How clever of you, Muggles! Now what were those other things, Walter the Earl—the things he said were in the chests?"

"Armor . . ." Walter the Earl wrinkled his brow. "Something to go on the arms?" He tapped the metal guards on his own arms. "Well, perhaps—"

A sudden loud pounding sounded from above, and the three froze in their places. Somebody was knocking at the door of Walter the Earl's house.

The candle fell from Curley Green's hand and went out. There was a pause, and then the pounding recommenced. If it was the town clerk . . . or the mayor, himself, returned from Watersplash . . .

The pounding stopped. Muggles scarcely breathed.

The silence went on so long that Walter the Earl's metal suit gave a relieved squeak, and Curley Green bent over cautiously to search for the candle. But a new sound stiffened them. Little clods of dirt came filtering down outside the narrow opening of the vault. Somebody was standing on top of the dirt pile.

There was a slipping and a sliding, and the next moment the light from the opening was blocked off. Muggles huddled inside the jeweled cloak to make herself look smaller, but she knew it was hopeless. Whoever was standing out there would be standing inside in a moment, and the secret of the treasures would be discovered.

Then a voice exclaimed:

> "Well, I'll be bound—
> He's underground!
> And what a pleasure—
> He's found the treasure!"

"Gummy!" Curley Green cried. "It's only Gummy!"

"At your service—don't be nervous!" The figure slipped through the aperture and made a low bow before them, sweeping off his tall conical hat. "Though what you mean by *only* Gummy, I can't imagine." As Curley Green lit the candle again, his eyes widened and he stared first at Walter the Earl's metal helmet, then at the three twinkling jeweled cloaks, and finally his gaze wandered over the iron chests scattered about the chamber. He gave a low whistle and suddenly clasped himself in a delighted hug that sent his sun-yellow cloak flying. "Oh joy, oh joy!" he cried, and then his eyes flew wide in consternation.

"Oh, my hat! Oh, my shoe!
Oh, my nose and ear!
You'd better find an exit quick—
The town clerk's nearly here!"

Curley Green jumped up in alarm. "But the treasure—"

Gummy nodded sadly. "Co.'s hopping mad. If we don't fill up that hole outside within *one* hour, he's going to put Walter the Earl out of his house. For good."

"Then the treasure will be lost again!" Muggles wrung her hands.

"Oh no, that's all right," said Walter the Earl. "We'll use the trapdoor."

"Trapdoor!" They stared at him blankly.

"Over there." Walter the Earl waved at the farthest corner. "I knew there must have been one. It was the first thing I looked for when I broke in."

With a bound, Gummy was across the room and scaling the metal rungs of the ladder fastened against the wall.

"You had better be careful," Walter the Earl warned. "I believe it opens onto—"

"Got it!" Gummy cried. He tugged at a latch in the ceiling and then stepped down a few rungs to let the trapdoor fall free. "Oogh!" he yelled as an avalanche of ashes cascaded over him.

"—onto my fireplace," Walter the Earl finished.

3

Trout made into fish cakes is still trout.

—Muggles, *Maxims*

When Muggles parted from her new friends two hours
later, she was almost bursting with excitement. It
was not until she reached the museum that she remembered why she had left it so hurriedly in the
first place. Her dream! She half turned back to catch
up with Gummy and Curley Green, but then she
saw Wm. the Official Village Poet bearing down on
the museum, and hastened ahead to be there before
him. Wm. was the prickly kind who made a fuss
about little things. Of course, he was very important,
and very important folk so often *were* prickly, in
Muggles's experience.

But she needn't have worried this morning, for
Wm. was in the throes of composing a welcoming
poem. He came muttering and mumbling through
the door, intent on the sheet of reed paper in one
hand. In the other he carried a sharpened wax-writer
with which he jabbed out the rhythm as he read:

"Ltd. had a little boat,
Its paint was silver-gray,
And everywhere that Ltd. went,
That boat took him away.

"It paddled him to Watersplash,
Full fifty miles upstream,
And then it brought him home again—

"Duh-*dum*-duh-*dum*-duh-*dream* . . .

"Duh-*dum*-duh-*dum*-duh-*seem* . . .

"Or scream," he muttered. "Scheme, theme, beam, team, gleam . . . Blister!"

"G-good morning," said Muggles breathlessly, with a look at the Fooley Poem to be sure it was hanging straight.

Wm. gave a jerk of surprise. "Oh . . . er . . . a very good morning to you." He started to bestow a smile upon her, but his eyes dropped to the orange sash, and the smile turned out to be a frown.

Muggles plucked at her cloak with nervous fingers to cover the offending sash. "Everybody is looking forward to your welcoming poem," she put in hastily. "Is it sad?"

"Sad?" said Wm. sharply. "Why *should* it be sad?"

"We-ell. . . ." Muggles hesitated timidly. "I just thought—well, you know, since the Fooley Poem is so sad, I thought maybe . . ."

"Nonsense. Clearly, you don't understand it."

"No, I don't think I do," Muggles answered humbly. "At least, I'm put off by some of the words. Lamb, for instance. I never can decide what a lamb looks like, unless it's a wood mouse with white fur." Wm. had begun to frown again, and Muggles rushed on in fright. "And then there's this queer word, 'school.' Why is it against the rule for a wood mouse to go there? I didn't think wood mice *had* any rules. And why weren't the children laughing and playing before the wood mouse came? If children don't laugh and play, it's almost certain they're ill, so I suppose school must be where you go when you're ill. So then this Mary person must have been ill, or she wouldn't be going to school, and altogether it's a sad sort of poem, isn't it?"

"Nonsense." He stared condescendingly down his pointed nose at her. "*Utter* nonsense. Look here!" He ran his finger under the first line of the Fooley Poem. " 'Mary had a little lamb.' A lamb is a friend, obviously. Mary had a little *friend*. Is there anything sad about that?"

Muggles shook her head.

" 'Its fleece was white as snow.' That's clear

enough. The little friend, instead of wearing a sensible, ordinary cloak of watercress-green"—and here Wm. looked pointedly at Muggles's orange sash— "instead of dressing in that beautiful Minnipin color, the little friend put on a garish, improper cloak of white and followed Mary into the meetinghouse, where he had no business, being too young to attend village meetings. 'It made the children laugh and play!' I don't wonder! Even the *children* of the village realized what an idiot Mary's friend was making of himself, and made fun of him for being so ridiculous. Quite right, too."

"You're quite wrong, you know," said a new voice.

Muggles and Wm. both turned. In the doorway, his gold-embroidered cloak glinting in the sun, stood Walter the Earl. He strode across the museum toward them, swinging the silvery ashplant which he always carried.

"Quite wrong, you know." He lifted the stick and tapped it against the poem on the wall. Wm. shuddered as though he had been struck, while Muggles hugged herself in delicious terror.

"Lamb," Walter the Earl went on, tapping the poem again. "Obviously a shortened spelling of lamprey. And a lamprey, as you know, is a sort of eel that fastens onto fish with its suckers and finally kills them. Therefore, Mary is a fish, which would account for the lamprey's following her, you see, wherever she goes." Once more he raised the ashplant, but Wm. caught it before it could touch the precious poem.

Walter the Earl scarcely noticed. "The word 'school' is of course more difficult unless one has studied the old language, as I have, and learned that a lot of fish swimming together was once known as a school of fish—what we call a gobble. So the lamprey hung on to Mary when she went to join her friends, and the children along the bank of the river thought it looked funny to see a lamprey in a gobble of fish."

As Wm. fastened his full attention upon the Fooley Poem, Walter the Earl delivered a large wink at Muggles, then grew stern once more.

"They are very stupid children to think it a laughing matter when a lamprey starts destroying their food. It's a silly poem. Doesn't make any more sense than that ridiculous thing called a painting." He waved the ashplant toward the opposite wall.

Muggles felt a giggle begin to rise in her throat. Of course, it was very wicked of Walter the Earl to say such things, almost as bad as laughing while Ltd. the Mayor made a speech, but Wm. looked so funny, almost as though he had a lamprey fastened to *him*. . . .

Wm. began to splutter. "Take care, you . . . Take care, I say . . . You'd better have a care, sir . . ."

"Bosh," said Walter the Earl. "Bosh and feathers!"

"I shall . . . Yes, I certainly shall . . ." Wm. gasped and gulped. "I *most* certainly shall report . . . Oh yes, indeed . . . yes . . . yes . . ." He turned and fled from the museum.

"Hah!" said Walter the Earl. "Vanquished without a stroke!"

"All the same," Muggles said reprovingly, "you really oughtn't to have said that about Fooley. It's not . . . not . . ." She felt the giggle rising again.

"My dear Muggles," and Walter the Earl drew his finger down his long stern nose, "my *dear* Muggles, aren't you weary of poems everlastingly and forevermore starting with 'Turkle had a little trout' or 'Bunty had a tiny house' simply because the Fool brought this Mary poem back with him?"

Muggles squirmed uncomfortably. "Well, I just supposed I wasn't clever enough to understand—"

"Exactly. And because you do understand Gummy's scribble, you think it must not be very good. Isn't that right?"

"Ye-es, but—" Muggles looked round anxiously. "Do you think you ought to call Fooley 'the Fool'? You never know—"

"Ah." Walter the Earl leaned closer, his hands folded over the knob of his ashplant. "That is what I came to tell you. A fact, my good Muggles, is a fact. And the fact about Fooley is that he didn't know a fin from a tail!"

Muggles's eyes flew wide. "But Fooley was wise! 'Fooley the wise and brave and good.' And his balloon—"

"*His* balloon!" Walter the Earl's great booming laugh bounced against the walls, setting the poem and the painting and the family tree to chattering in their frames. "*His* balloon happened to be made by the village toymaker for a fun fair."

Muggles glanced uneasily at the open door. "But—but how do you know?"

"It's all in the scrolls. Facts, Muggles, facts! Fooley had nothing to do with that balloon, except that he sneaked a ride before it was properly tied down. So instead of just rising as high as the tallest trees, he kept right on going—squalling at the top of his lungs, I might add. Muggles, this great ancestor, this worshipful forebear of Wm. and Ltd. and Co. and all the rest of the Periods, was called the

Fool because that is exactly what he was! Now, there is a good honest fact for you!"

"Oh hush, please," Muggles begged him. "Somebody will hear!"

And indeed, there was a shout outside in the marketplace, followed by a muttering and a murmuring and a swelling of voices. Footsteps pattered on the cobblestones.

"Now you've done it," Muggles cried. "You'd better hide." She looked round in desperation. There wasn't a nook or a cranny big enough to hold him.

"Did my forebear Walter the Obtuse hide?" Walter the Earl demanded.

"He hid the swords and things, didn't he?" retorted Muggles.

Walter the Earl stood unconvinced, while the voices outside got louder and more excited.

"Here," Muggles urged, seizing the folds of Fooley's balloon. "Here, crawl under this, and I'll say—"

But he drew himself up to his fullest height and struck the floor imperiously with his ashplant. "Walter the Earl is not a worm that crawls!" Swinging his cloak back over his shoulders, he advanced toward the door to reveal himself to the outraged Minnipins in the marketplace. Muggles trailed fearfully behind him and peeped over his shoulder at the gathering throng.

But they were paying no attention to the museum or Walter the Earl or Muggles. In the very center of the marketplace stood that lamppost where Etc.'s reed-light burned at night, and tacked on the post was a notice, newly put up by the official village painter, whose spelling was even worse when he was in a hurry.

Everybody Notice

A message has been received by Special Boat that Ltd. the Mayor will not return until tomorrow and then will make an Important Announcement affecting everybody. Grand Holiday Proclamed!

4

If you don't look for Trouble,
how can you know it's there?

—Muggles, *Maxims*

There was no more work done that morning in Slip-per-on-the-Water. Excited villagers clustered in the marketplace to talk about the extraordinary message from Ltd.

In the flurry Muggles lost sight of Walter the Earl. *I must find out about my dream*, she thought, *but every time I am about to ask, something else happens.* She pushed her way through the chattering crowds, looking for Gummy or Curley Green, but she looked in vain. Every cloak behind every other cloak was a good grave green like her own. Finally, she gave up and went home to put a pot of turtle soup on the fire. But just as it had simmered the right amount of time, there was a tap on her door.

Mingy the Money Keeper stood on the doorstone, scowling fiercely and clutching his money box to his chest. There was a brand-new lock on it.

"Co. said there are to be free gob-stoppers for the children tomorrow," he snapped. "Free! Just because the money comes out of this box, he calls it free." Mingy gave the money box a shake. It had a comfortable fat chunky sound. "That's not all. . . . May I come in?"

Muggles stepped back to admit him. "I've got a savory little pot of turtle soup just ready for eating," she said. "And I do like a bit of company. Now let me see, where is that other stool? Ah, there it is!" She scooped up a massive heap of odds and ends, and revealed a rickety stool. "It won't hold me— that's why I keep it covered up, so I won't sit on it by mistake—but a little thin thing like you will be all right. You don't eat enough, Mingy, and that's the truth. Now, where is my ladle?" She pressed a finger against the tip of her nose and thought. "Of course!" With a swoop, she delved into the hearthstone pile and emerged waving the ladle triumphantly. "Now, sit down, Mingy, and put your money box under the table where you're sure to find it again, and we'll have some soup and a good fresh loaf, sping-spang right on the spot!"

Before he knew quite what had happened, Mingy was sitting across from her, spooning the savory turtle soup and eating crunchy slices of bread, thickly buttered. Before very long, just as she knew it would, his face began to crack into an unaccustomed smile.

"I do like to watch folk eat," Muggles went on, "but most of the time there's just me to watch, so you can see what a pleasure it is to set good soup in front of somebody else."

"Yes. Well . . ." And Mingy reached for another slice of bread. Midway through it, he began to scowl again. "Gob-stoppers!" he burst out. "Fresh paint for the merry-go-long! And now a banner saying 'Welcome home Ltd.' to be strung up on the dock! There's no end to it." He took a savage bite out of the bread. "But there'll be an end to the gold one of these days, I can tell you that." The stool squeaked alarmingly as he jumped up to stride up and down the room, waving the piece of bread in the air. "And I so much as propose a sick fund, what happens? *You* know what happened last meeting!"

"I know, Mingy, I know," Muggles said soothingly. "About the gob-stoppers . . . I was thinking maybe something a little bit different, as a special treat—"

"Doesn't matter, but don't expect any extra money for it." He turned his stride so quickly that he almost fell over one of Muggles's piles. "What's this I hear about you hobnobbing with Them?" he demanded. "You lost your senses?"

"N-no. I wasn't hobnobbing. . . . I was just—"

"Well, best stop it, whatever you were *just*." He caught sight of what he was waving in the air and took another bite of it. "Not that I care whether you're seen coming out of Walter the Earl's house, it's nothing to *me*. But Wm. is flapping his tongue all over the marketplace . . ."

"Wm.!"

". . . talking about disloyalty and I don't know what all. Walter the Earl should be outlawed, he is saying."

"Outlawed!"

"Don't keep repeating words after me, it's annoying. Outlawed, I said. And Co. is muttering against Gummy. Says he's a troublemaker. So you'd best keep away before you get mixed up in something. Wm.'s dangerous, he is."

"But I—Mingy, let me tell you something—"

"Oh no, tell me nothing. I've got troubles of my own. Got to be going now." Mingy stuffed the last of the bread into his mouth and started to pick up his money box, then put it down again. "Like to borrow some candle molds for Spill. The old clumsy has broken his last one and what good is the village candlemaker without a mold? While you're looking, might as well mend your rickety stool. Wretched thing all but dumped me on the floor."

A few minutes later, the stool once more firm on its legs, Mingy took his leave with four candle molds Muggles had found in her heaps. "Can't promise you'll ever get them back. Don't forget to make the gob-stoppers or whatever. And mind you stay away from Them. There's no trouble like trouble."

There's no trouble like trouble, Muggles repeated to herself, as she cleared the table. *I'll forget about the—the dream, and the treasure.* Resolutely, she began to collect the materials for the gob-stoppers or whatever. Gob-stoppers were rather dull to make, but little mint-candy folk . . . She could call them Mintypins! Humming a made-up tune, she set a pot of syrup to boil, to which she added a few drops of her mint essence, and all the while that she was stirring and adding ingredients, she managed to keep her thoughts on the important announcement instead of on Them.

When she came to pour out the stiffened mixture in the shape of Mintypins, however, she was dissatisfied. They looked so unfinished, not at all as she had imagined them. Humming a different tune, she measured out more ingredients and began to experiment with candy clothes for the Mintypins. These she spread on with a knife, and the result looked a little like Walter the Earl in the metal suit.

If there were long knives and the snouted hats with plumes . . .

An hour later she surveyed the trays of Minty-pins with pride. Suits and hats of golden taffy, plumes of spun sugar, long knives of—*I'll call that sword-stick*, she decided. She ran her finger along the tiny blade. *I wonder if it really is a sword*, she mused, *and if Walter the Earl has found out the secret. If I do as Mingy said, I'll probably never know, unless . . . unless . . .* And again the sharp pictures of her dream flashed into her head. The dream . . . Walter the Earl's pit . . . the fleeting glimpse of Curley Green's blob . . .

She snatched up her cloak. One more little visit to Walter the Earl's house couldn't get her into trouble. Besides, she had promised to give him some polish. But the chief reason for going—and it had been preying on her mind even as she thought of other things—was that if there was talk of outlawing Walter the Earl, it was only fair that Walter the Earl should be warned!

Clasping the clay jar of polish in her arms, she crossed the marketplace. Was it her imagination, or did some of the green-cloaked figures turn away at her approach? *I've done nothing wrong*, she told herself, but even so, her heart hammered almost as loudly as her tap on Walter the Earl's door. When it was flung open, she was glad enough to slip inside out of sight of prying eyes.

"There's no doubt about it," Walter the Earl exclaimed, as he drew Muggles in, "the black knife *is* a sword. I haven't discovered the secret yet, but I've come across things like 'flashing swords' and 'righteous swords gleaming, their blinding light a curse upon the enemy!' And look here!" He snatched up a scroll from the litter around his chair, rapidly unrolling it. "What do you think of this!"

"Why, it's a painting!" Muggles cried. "That is—but it's much bigger than Fooley's painting, and it's got queer writing on it. What does it say?"

"I don't know yet," Walter the Earl confessed. "The writing is of an even more ancient script than the other things. But here is something else." He plucked another scroll out of the heap and unwound it before Muggles's eyes.

It was a blob—a picture of a marketplace that could easily have been Slipper-on-the-Water except that it was much larger—and the houses! There seemed to be hundreds of them in the background. They rose, tier on tier, up the side of a slope. But the thing that caught Muggles's attention and held it was the figures in the foreground. There were some green cloaks, it is true, but they were almost lost in the reds and yellows and oranges and browns.

And some of the Minnipins were dressed in the metal suits and jeweled cloaks that were now in the vault below Muggles's very feet!

Walter the Earl pointed to the script at the bottom of the picture. " 'Golden Mountain, Home of the Minnipins,' " he translated. "Don't you see, it's where Gammage came from—where we all came from! Wait until Ltd. sees this—*after* I've deciphered all the manuscripts, of course." He dropped his voice. "We must move with caution, Muggles. The Periods are not going to like these discoveries."

Muggles suddenly remembered her errand. "That's why I've come," she said. "They don't like it already. Walter the Earl, Wm. is going to make trouble. He says you are disloyal—you know, because of what you said in the museum—and . . . Please listen!"

But Walter the Earl only gave an absent nod. He had picked up another scroll and was already lost in deciphering its contents.

"You must listen! Wm. is saying you should be outlawed!"

"Mmmm, yes." He sank into his chair, brows knit over the faded writing. " 'Once again,' " he read slowly, " 'the Big Ones of the Mushroom Color' . . . mmm . . . 'were . . . were dispelled? . . . repelled? . . . repulsed,' that's it, 'but always

they came back, loving' . . . mmm . . . 'loving over-
much the . . . wealth of gold in the Minnipin . . .
city, but each time they were . . . were vanquished
by our . . . by our valiant Minnipin . . . warriors
with their slashing swords of light . . .' " His voice
sank to a mumble.

Muggles tried one last time, her voice loud.
"This morning I saw something on the mountain, or
I *think* I did, and . . ." It was no use. Walter the
Earl wouldn't have heard a thunderbolt. Muggles
let herself out of the house and stood uncertainly
on the doorstone. Should she go to Gummy's house
and ask him about the dream? Several passersby

gave her curious looks, but it was not until Co. came along that she stepped down hastily and started across the marketplace. She could feel that he had stopped and was staring after her. *I don't dare go to Gummy's now*, she thought, *not with Co. watching*.

But then she had a new thought. Gummy was more often than not to be found lying under a tree along the riverbank. If she were to take a basket and gather cowslips for cowslip conserve . . .

She found Gummy at last, but not before she had gathered a goodly supply of the little flowers and jumped a dozen times at the eerie sounds of the woods. He was stretched out flat under a sycamore, his conical hat over his face.

"Hello," said Muggles.

Gummy held up his hand for silence without removing the hat.

> "Bright sunshine,
> Blue flowers,
> Pink rainbows,
> Moisty showers.
>
> Spring ting-a-ling!
> Ting-a-ling spring!"

The hat rose and fell with the words. "Or do you

prefer something like . . . hmmm . . . Muggles . . .
Muggles . . .

"Muggles, when she makes a dash,
Struggles with her orange sash.
Folk should never stop to twiddle
With what they've got around their middle."

Then, with one gliding motion, he was on his feet.
"Muggles, my good friend, what brings you here
where the sun is shining clear?"

"Well, it's . . ." Suddenly, Muggles felt embarrassed. Of course her dream was just a dream!
But Gummy was waiting with his head cocked to
one side to hear her out. She plunged her hand into
the cowslips, turning them over. "It's just that I've
been thinking about something Walter the Earl said
this morning. He said we don't know what's going
on outside the valley. And then that parchment he
read to us—all about how the treasures would be
found when they were needed, and—well, it's enough
to make a body reflect, isn't it?"

"It is," Gummy said, giving his hat a thoughtful
twirl.

"You talked to Co. about it this morning, didn't
you? That's why he got so angry."

"Yes," said Gummy slowly, "I did mention

something of the sort to our worthy town clerk. But 'Nonsense,' said he. 'Some more of your trickery,' said he. 'Nobody can get into the valley, and nobody can get out of the valley, and don't you go stirring up trouble or I'll stir you up some *real* trouble,' said he. Anyway," Gummy finished cheerfully, clapping his hat on his head, "it doesn't matter. Co. was right. No one—even those Mushrooms Walter the Earl is so fond of talking about—can come over the Sunset Mountains without arriving with a broken neck. I give you my word on that. Why, you get a crick in your back just *looking* up the side of those cliffs. So if there's anybody lurking on the top of the Sunset Mountains, they'll just have to lurk in the murk until they get tired and go back home."

Muggles gave up twiddling with the cowslips in her basket and looked him squarely in the eye. "It *wasn't* a dream, was it?"

Gummy gave a start. "What wasn't a dream?"

"Seeing you go across the marketplace early this morning all dripping wet, and talking with Walter the Earl, and pointing up at the . . . the thing I thought was the sunrise on the Sunset Mountains." Her eyes accused him. "You were coming from your other house up the Little Trickle because you had seen the . . . the sunrise . . . only you knew it wasn't the sunrise . . ." Her voice faltered, then steadied. "It's fires on top of the mountains, isn't it? There is somebody or something up there, and they're trying to get into our valley. That's why you talked to Co., but Co. wouldn't believe you. So it wasn't a dream at all, was it?"

"No," said Gummy softly. "Odd as it may seem, your dream was not a dream."

5

WELCUM HOME! in Geo.'s script
Cost a gold-bit and got ripped.
WELCOME HOME! in voices swelling
Is cheaper and—much better spelling!

—Gummy, *Scribbles*
(Collected Works)

The quiet plash of the Watercress River sounded loud in Muggles's ears. Overhead a small bird whistled and was answered farther downstream.

"It was my leaky roof," Gummy explained. "I was sleeping in my fine stone house way up the Little Trickle, and the wet and the dry of it is that when it rained last night, it rained right through the roof onto *me*. So I got up and lit the fire to dry me out, and when I happened to look out the window, I saw the fires on the mountains—"

"But what did you think?"

"Think? Why, I didn't really think at all. I just hopped into my boat and set myself afloat—"

"But why didn't you go straight to Co.? If he had seen the fires, he would have to believe you!"

Gummy grinned. "Would *you* like to wake up Co. in the middle of the night? What a plight!"

"No-o," Muggles admitted. She thought a moment. "Then you told Walter the Earl, and he started right in to dig for the—the swords and things. But how did he know just where to dig?"

"Inspiration, *he* called it." Gummy picked a cowslip out of the basket and put it on his tongue. "I myself think it was simply the only place left." He pulled out the blossom and squinted at it thoughtfully.

"I wonder why a cow should slip,
And how a grass can hopper . . ."

"And what are you going to do about it?" demanded Muggles.

"That doesn't rhyme, and the line's too long," Gummy said.

"Or when—"

"I said, what are you going to do about it?"
He looked at her blankly. "Do about what? Oh.

Oh, you mean the fires. Well, I've done it. I told Co., didn't I? What else?

"Or when the butter fills a cup . . ."

Muggles snatched the cowslip away from him. "Why won't you be serious? You must tell Ltd. tomorrow, of course! And tonight—" She fixed him with a stern eye. "Tonight you will have to watch for the fires again, and this time if you see them, you must go straight to Co., no matter what hour it is!"

Gummy gave a resigned sigh. "Very well, I'll try to do both, if you'll just go away now and let me finish my rhyme in peace." He plucked another cowslip from her basket. "Now where was I . . . ?"

But there were no fires that night. Muggles, sure that Gummy would never stay awake under a sound roof, kept watch herself, sitting up through the long hours wrapped in her comforter, with an occasional pot of hot sassafras tea to warm her chilled bones. The reed-light flickered in the empty marketplace, and not a sound disturbed the night. Finally, at dawn, she dozed off, to awaken shortly with a crick in her neck and the irritable feeling that her vigil had been a piece of folly. *Getting into such a stew when nobody else is worried is stupid,* she scolded herself. *The proper place for a stew is in the pot.* Feeling weary, she took herself off to the museum, where she cleaned with such fury that the dust made her cough.

When she emerged once more, the marketplace was a-clatter with preparations for the holiday of Ltd.'s homecoming. Loaf the Baker and Thatch the Roofer were putting up bobble-boards and dizzy-swings for the children. Thum, the miller's assistant, was hooking together the four carts of the merry-go-long—the silver trout, the green-and-brown turtle, the balloon basket, and the watercress plant. In the middle of the square Fin Longtooth, the oldest inhabitant, had set up his fishing tank and was now stocking it with fish netted from the Watercress. The village children—

With a shocked gasp, Muggles stopped short beside the fishing tank.

The village children were clustered under Walter the Earl's family tree, watching openmouthed as Walter the Earl made slashing motions with one of the blackened swords from the treasure.

"Tell us again about the evil Mushrooms!" the children shrilled.

I must stop him, Muggles thought desperately. *I must not get mixed up with Them anymore*, she thought again.

"If you're looking for advice," Fin muttered in her ear, "you'll keep clear of that one and the rest of Them. They're nothing but trouble and more trouble."

"But I—"

"Muggles! Ho, there!" Dingle the Miller came puffing across the marketplace from the Street Going to the River. "Co. wants a bit of string down at the dock. Hurry! He's in a state. They're putting up Geo.'s new banner!"

"Cost a gold-bit, too, they say." Fin smacked his lips. "And they tell me . . ."

But Muggles had already set off for her house to get the string. *He wouldn't listen anyway, Walter the Earl wouldn't. He's hopeless!*

The dock was aswarm with villagers draping fresh garlands from post to post. Over their heads Geo. the Official Village Painter and his cousin Bros. teetered on ladders with a great flapping banner stretched between them—WELCUM HOME LTD., it proclaimed in Geo.'s best script.

Then suddenly, just as Muggles rounded the corner of the Street Going to the River, Bros.'s ladder gave a lurch, and Bros. let go of his end of the banner. With a snap, it recoiled and wrapped itself around Geo.'s head. Geo. staggered, clawed with one leg at the ladder, missed, and, arms and legs flying in all directions, landed on the dock with a resounding thump.

For a moment nobody moved, and then, with Geo.'s first strangled scream, green cloaks fluttered and flapped as the villagers all rushed to help. Muggles began to run.

"I can't see!" Geo. shouted in a queer muffled voice. "The light has gone from my eyes!"

"Where's that Muggles?" Co. roared. "Geo.'s badly hurt!"

Tremblingly, Muggles pushed past Co.'s terrible glare and knelt beside the thrashing official village painter.

"Can't see!" Geo. yelled through the folds of the banner. "Can't breathe!"

"Lie still." Muggles grasped his flailing arms. "Somebody unwrap his head."

Mingy, who was nearest, put his money box down, sat on it, and began to unwind the WELCUM banner. "Hold still," he ordered. "I'm not paying out a gold-bit for another one of these."

Co. rubbed his bald head distractedly. "This is all your fault, Muggles!" he stormed. "I send for a bit of string, and where are you? Off hobbing and nobbing with blobs and scribbles so you can't be found. While poor Geo. . . . ."

"That's not true." Curley Green's clear voice cut across Co.'s furious tones. "She hasn't been near us all the morning. Besides, you only sent for her a minute ago."

Co.'s wrath, diverted from Muggles, fell full upon Curley Green. "And what have you been doing while honest folk toil? Let me see that!" He snatched the piece of birch bark from her fingers and turned it over.

It was a picture of the dock scene, full of busy green cloaks. And there was Geo. on the ladder, teetering wildly, his head swathed in the flapping banner on which only the word WELCUM was visible.

"Give me that!" Geo. suddenly cried. He pushed Mingy and Muggles away and sprang to his feet, trailing folds of cloth from his ears. "Give me that— that *thing!* " For a moment he stared at the blob, his face crimson, and then he dashed it to the ground and stamped on it.

There was a stunned silence while openmouthed villagers stood waiting for the next move.

"Back to work," Co. snapped. "Curley Green, I forbid you to paint any more blobs. I *forbid* you! And as for you, Muggles"—he turned his furious

gaze on her—"go home and take off that ridiculous sash!"

"I'll not do it! I have a right to wear what I please!" But Muggles only said it to herself when she was well out of earshot of the town clerk.

Of course, she did take off the sash. No use throwing the door wide open when trouble was standing just outside. Besides, it needed a good sudsing. So she washed it and hung it up to dry. Then she uncovered the pans of candy she had made yesterday, and transferred the Mintypins to one big tray, not without a qualm as she saw how realistic the swords and armor looked.

"Nonsense," she scoffed, "they're only candy. Licked down in a minute by small pink tongues and no harm done."

She hurried through her midday meal, for already she could hear the holiday-makers gathering in the marketplace, and the reed pipes were playing snatches of tunes. There was nothing so gay as a clear reed pipe to set one's feet to tapping, and Muggles began to cheer up for the first time that day. Ltd. would soon be back, and everything would straighten itself out.

Outside, the reeds piped louder. Snatching up the tray, she was halfway through the door when she looked back at the orange sash fluttering dry before the window. *Co. said I should take it off, and I've taken it off*, she thought. *If I should put it back on now . . . It's not as if it was just an ordinary day . . . A bright sash is only a sort of garland, after all . . . And there's nothing wrong with garlands . . .*

A moment later she emerged into the festive air of the marketplace. Between Fooley Hall and the museum the pipers played jaunty tunes for fast dancing, and between the mayor's house and Supplys more pipers trilled in slower time for the slow dancing. There were games of ringtoss and pegboard, and for the more sedate villagers games of "What Am I Thinking About?" And all the while the bobble-boards bobbled, the dizzy-swings swung, and Thum, the miller's assistant, made chuffing puffing noises as he pulled cargoes of children around the sides of the square in the merry-go-long.

In no time at all the Mintypins on Muggles's tray had been claimed by the children, and she hurried to join the rest of the merrymakers, the orange streamers of her sash swinging out with the fast dancing and fluttering with the slow. It was a holiday to make the glummest heart glad, this homecoming celebration for the mayor. Even Co. unbent enough to enter the slow dancing.

Everything is going to be all right, Muggles thought as she threaded her way to the fringes of the crowd to catch her breath. "Everything is going to be *quite* all right," she repeated aloud.

"And has anything been wrong?" inquired a voice in her ear.

Startled, Muggles looked up into the face of— Ltd.!

Ltd.! Muggles blinked, but when she looked again, he was still standing there, grave and plump, every hair of his long mayoral beard whisked into place, as though he had never been away.

"But you're not—you shouldn't be—"

"Ah, but I am. I had a fast current." Ltd. patted down a wisp of beard that began to stray in the breeze. "Now, what is this about everything going to be all right?"

"Well, I—I hardly know," said Muggles in confusion. "It was so strange, you see, that I was sure I was dreaming, only I wasn't." She plunged quickly into the tale of what she had seen yesterday morning, talking fast to keep Ltd.'s eyes from straying past her to the festive crowd.

When she paused for breath, he gave an absent nod. "Yes, yes," he murmured. "We all have bad dreams, but it's nothing to be disturbed about. Eat less heavily at supper and—" His eyes dropped to the orange sash about her waist. "I think, Muggles . . ."

But she never heard what the mayor thought, for suddenly Ltd.'s presence was discovered by the others.

"There's Ltd.!" somebody cried, and the next thing Muggles knew she had been swept away from the mayor's side. Cries of "It's Ltd.!" and "Ltd.'s come back!" went up on all sides.

"Important announcement, everybody," cried Co. importantly.

A hand shot out to steady Muggles as she stumbled in the backwash of the crowd.

"You might stop by me," Mingy said gruffly, "unless you find a good honest green cloak too dull for you these days."

Muggles gave him a reproachful look, but he

only rattled his money box in a reassuring sort of way. "Don't like the smell of this important announcement we're going to hear, and that's the truth. Mark you, before the day is over, Ltd. will be tapping at the money box." And Mingy beat a brisk tattoo on the lid.

Ltd. had been carried along by the throng and thrust up on a box in the very center of the marketplace. Now he raised his hand, and immediately the excited clamor was stilled.

"Good villagers," he began, smoothing his beard, "I shall not keep you wondering what the promised important announcement is by making a long speech at this time. Good folk, I bring you great and good news. There is going to be a contest—village against village!"

A murmur of excitement swept through the crowd. Mingy took a firmer hold on his money box, and his mouth set in a grim line.

Ltd. went on, patting his beard. "Tomorrow morning three good citizens of Watersplash will set out to visit each village for a day and a night, but in what order nobody knows except themselves. These three judges will decide which of the villages is the most prosperous, the happiest, the prettiest—in short, the *finest* village in the Land Between the Mountains. And—" Here Ltd. lowered his voice. "—I am confident that if we all work together to get ready for this inspection, there can be no doubt which village will win the prize!"

There was a burst of enthusiastic clapping. Muggles clasped Mingy's arm in delight. But Mingy shook her off.

"If you please, Ltd.," he called out above the hubbub, "what exactly do you mean by 'getting ready for the inspection'?"

"Ah," said Ltd., combing his beard with his fingers, "cleaning and polishing and sweeping, roofs mended and houses painted—"

"But we painted last year. This year the money—"

"Whose money is it?" demanded Co. "Mingy's or the village's?"

"That's right!"

"Don't pay attention to—"

Mingy rattled his money box warningly. "It won't be *anybody's* when it's all gone!"

"Mingy always spoils everything," Bros. sneered. "What good is gold if it's always locked up in a box?"

The mayoral brow creased in a frown as he looked over the angry faces before him. "If the judges were here right now," he said, "what would they think of Slipper-on-the-Water?"

There was an uncomfortable silence.

"I see that my point is well made," Ltd. went on quietly. "Are there any more objections before I continue?"

Feet scuffed the cobblestones in embarrassment. Nobody said anything for several moments, though Mingy made a low growling sound, and Muggles held her breath lest he break out afresh.

But the voice that spoke up at last came from a new quarter. "If you please, Ltd.," said Walter the Earl in his most ringing tones, "I have no objections to painting houses, but something has happened that everybody should know about, something more important than foolish contests. Yesterday morning, before the sun rose—"

"Just a moment!" Co. snapped. "Walter the Earl is going to tell you a story which I have already heard and investigated. Gummy would have us believe that he spent the night before last sleeping out in the rain, and when he woke up, he saw an orange light like fire on the mountains. Then, so he says, he paddled his boat home in the middle of the night, in the rain—this is *Gummy*, mind you, who hasn't the energy to polish his own doorknob for your homecoming. And when he got Walter the Earl out of bed—why Walter the Earl? Why not me?—when he got his *crony* up to look at his orange light, the light disobligingly disappeared. No doubt it will reappear, however, in one of those famous scribbles!"

There was a spurt of nervous laughter, which died away immediately. Ltd. shot a glance at Muggles over the heads of the crowd, and Muggles, trembling, spoke up for the first time in public.

"I saw it, too," she quavered.

Ltd. broke the strained silence that followed her words. "Surely you told me it was a dream?"

"No, I—" Muggles's voice almost failed her. "I thought it was a dream, but later when I talked to Gummy—"

"You see!" Co. cried triumphantly. "Gummy again! Always Gummy! He has played on poor simple Muggles's fears until she will believe anything! But lest anybody else fall a victim to this trickster's pranks, let me tell you that at the loss of a good night's sleep, I have proved him a fraud. I stayed awake until dawn this morning, watching the Sunset Mountains. And I can report that there wasn't so much as a falling star to disturb the skyline!"

Relief rippled through the square in a long-drawn sigh.

Walter the Earl thumped his ashplant on the floor. "But it wasn't raining last night, and—"

"Hoh!" Wm. cried. "Next you'll be saying it takes water to start a fire!"

At this there was an explosion of laughter that made the bobble-boards bobble.

Ltd. stamped his foot for order. "Let us hear what Gummy has to say for himself." He scanned the audience. "Will you speak up, Gummy?"

Everybody craned his neck for a sight of the sun-yellow cloak. Then, as it became apparent that there was no such cloak in the marketplace, the momentary silence broke into a twittering and a buzzing.

"He's not here!" Geo. exclaimed.

"Of course not!" jeered his wife Eng. "He's hiding his head in his bedclothes."

"Or up on the mountains, setting fire to the rocks!"

"He's pouring on water to make a good blaze!"

Ltd. smiled patiently until the laughter had subsided. "And now—the prize!"

For a moment Muggles was almost ready to believe that she had indeed dreamed the fires and that Gummy had somehow—but he *couldn't* know what she had dreamed! She held on to that tiny fact like a wood mouse clinging to a piece of bark aswirl in the Watercress.

"Yes, the prize!"

"The prize!"

Ltd. beamed on the villagers. "The prize, yes. The prize which we hope to win—which we *must* win!" He lowered his voice. "This prize, then, is the most precious object in the Land Between the Mountains, something which you have never seen because it has always remained in Watersplash since Gammage carried it to that place."

There was one startled exclamation and then a breathless hush as the villagers waited for his next words.

Ltd. nodded. "The prize, wrapped in the finest reed-silk to preserve its golden luster, will be borne by the judges on their journey, to be left at the village most worthy of the honor." He paused again, and a soft sigh rippled through the square. Ltd. brought his voice still lower until it was the barest sound. "The prize, my good folk, is nothing more nor less than that famous vessel of wisdom—the Gammage Cup!"

Then such a cheer went up that the dizzy-swings began to turn of themselves. Co. threw an arm about Walter the Earl's shoulders before he realized who it was. Even Mingy allowed a faint smile to creep into his granite face, and Muggles, her fears swallowed up by visions of beholding the venerated Gammage Cup, could only think—*It will surely be put in the museum and I—I shall touch it every day*! Dingle the Miller started a song, and the villagers joined in, at first raggedly, but all coming together for the chorus:

> Here's to our mayor,
> Good Ltd. the fair,
> Ltd. the wise
> With far-seeing eyes,
> Oh, here's to Ltd. the rare!

The reed pipes took up the tune, and toes began tapping. As the throng surged away from the mayor's box, Muggles's eyes met Ltd.'s over their heads. But in exchange for her smile, he gave her a somber, brooding look.

6

When you say what you think, be
sure to think what you say.

—Muggles, *Maxims*

The village was astir at dawn the next morning. By
order of the mayor, Splash the Painter and his sons
were set to work mixing great vats of lime and water
for whitewash, and smaller vats of flax oil and green
pigment with which to cover every door in the village. Thatch the Roofer climbed briskly over the
top of the mayor's house, replacing the dried reeds
where it was needed, and trimming the shaggy over-
hanging fringe into neat scallops. Blaze the Fire
Fighter was appointed to the new post of village
pruner, and went from family tree to family tree,
trimming and whacking. In the baker's shop, Loaf
experimented with a new recipe for making cakes,
while Dingle the Miller ground the special reed plant
finer than it had been ever been ground before, and
then ground it over again until he was whiter than

he had ever been before. Slipper-on-the Water hummed like a hive.

Muggles hummed right along with the rest of the village, but as she dismantled her heaps, dusted the articles, and carefully built them up again into tidier piles, she stopped frequently to look out the window. *It's none of my business, and I'd best stay out of it,* she told herself each time. *He's probably missed lots of meetings and nobody ever noticed before.*

But by the middle of the morning when the inside of her cottage was neat and tidy with all the piles re-sorted, Muggles slipped outside. Gummy's house had a closed secretive look, and anyway she had no intention of exposing herself to Co.'s wrath by going there. Instead, she set off for the riverbanks where she had found Gummy two days ago. But though she walked fearfully along the strip of woods as far as the Little Trickle, she found no sign of Gummy. Perplexed and uneasy, she walked back toward the dock.

Only then did it occur to her to look for Gummy's boat. Hastening her step, she scanned the boats tied up along the bank. The bright yellow craft was missing!

At first she felt relief. Gummy had only gone off

on one of his expeditions. Then a new uneasiness seized her. Supposing he had gone to the mountains? Supposing—

"Suppose nothing," she said shortly. "For all I know, Gummy is missing most of the time. He's completely undependable. I wash my hands of him." And she went back to the marketplace to claim her share of the paint.

As the day wore on and the cottages gleamed whiter and whiter, and their doors greener and greener, more and more often the villagers turned from their work to glance speculatively at the scarlet door that fronted on the marketplace. It remained scarlet; in fact, the more green paint that was splashed about on the other doors, the more scarlet Curley Green's door seemed to become. One of Splash's sons turned up with a ladder in midafternoon and coated the walls of her house with whitewash, but when he had finished and been paid by Curley Green, who appeared briefly to inspect his work, the door was still scarlet.

At last, just before teatime, that scarlet door, now watched by everybody within spying distance, opened, and Curley Green emerged with a pot of paint and a brush. A collective sigh went up, so heartfelt that it sounded like the wind in the trees. And Curley Green began to paint her door.

She painted it scarlet.

Eng., the wife of Geo., stared openmouthed across the marketplace and then turned to Muggles, who was whitewashing her own house in order to save her scarce gold pieces. "Do you see what she is doing!"

"It's her door," said Muggles, and got down to move her mended stool to another spot.

"But the Gammage Cup!" cried Eng., wringing her hands. "What will the judges think!"

Muggles turned round to face Eng. Queer—she had never before realized how much alike all the Periods looked. "Perhaps," she said slowly, "perhaps the judges will *like* it."

Eng. came as close as she ever would to being speechless. "Who ever heard of a Minnipin liking anything but a green door! It's ridiculous!"

"Well . . ." Muggles got up on her stool again. She knew that she had best agree with Eng. and let it go at that, but a small voice inside her head goaded her. *Go on*, it said, *go on and say it.*

"Well," Muggles said again, "well, that's not *quite* true. I mean, you must admit that Curley Green, at least, prefers scarlet, else she wouldn't paint her door that color. And I—" she hesitated and swallowed nervously. "And I—" She swallowed once more, and then gasped out, "I like it myself!" In a gesture of defiance, she sploshed her brush into the pail of whitewash and began spreading it on the wall in great swipes. She could feel Eng.'s unbelieving eyes boring into her, but she set her lips in a stubborn line. For the first time since she could remember, she had told a Period exactly what she thought, instead of what *they* thought she ought to think.

At last the long day of scrubbing and polishing and painting was over. When Brush appeared to give the cobblestones their nightly sweeping, folk walked about the square, admiring their shining village, calling out to each other in tired happy voices.

Muggles slipped over to the museum to see that all was in order; but she had no more than got inside when Walter the Earl appeared in the doorway. There was a suppressed air of excitement about him.

"Muggles!" he burst out. "When the Fool's balloon crashed and everything got scattered, how did the villagers know what was what when they picked the things up?"

"They—they matched them up with Fooley's list—the list he'd made in his book."

"Just so. Now look here!" He whipped a scroll from under his arm, opened it with a snap to show the circles and squares and shields. "What do you think this is?"

"Why, it's the painting I saw at your house." Muggles glanced uneasily past him. "Don't you think you'd better close the door?"

"Bother the door! Just look at this!" He pointed to the inscription that ran along the top of the scroll. "That says 'The Family Tree of the Ancient Line of Earls of Golden Mountain.' Do you hear that? The family tree! It's the history of a family!" He pointed a scornful finger at the wall where the picture of the willow tree hung. "*That's* not a family tree!"

"But—but what is it?" Muggles asked, bewildered.

"It's a painting!" Walter the Earl's voice rose triumphantly. "The villagers made a mistake! Because they had never heard of a family tree, and they didn't know a painting was just another name for a blob!" He stalked over to the wall.

"What are you going to do?" Muggles asked in alarm.

"Put things right. Correct the mistake. What else?" With a jerk, he removed the name placards from beneath the two frames and switched them.

"Put those back!" commanded a furious voice.

Muggles whirled round in fright.

There, standing in the doorway and white with rage, was the town clerk!

"Oh," Muggles gasped. She shrank away as Co. advanced threateningly into the room.

"Put those back!" he repeated. "And I'll take that trumped-up scroll you are flourishing so grandly."

Walter the Earl stared at him for a moment and then, with great deliberation, he stuck the parchment in his belt and folded his arms defiantly over it.

"Very well." Co. folded his own arms over his important paunch. "You will answer to the Council of Periods for this. As town clerk, I now declare the museum closed to you. You will leave *at once*."

Tremblingly, Muggles watched Walter the Earl stride out the door, his fearless figure quite unbent by Co.'s scathing look.

"Now then, Muggles," said Co. in a kinder voice, "you will please me by restoring those placards to their rightful places."

"B-but they are . . ." Muggles's protest died before the ice in Co.'s eyes. "Y-yes, Co."

"And now, Muggles," he said when she had done as he ordered, "I am not going to ask you to explain *this*," and he opened his hand to disclose a sticky, somewhat sucked Mintypin. "It is clear that Walter the Earl put you up to it—"

Muggles stiffened. "Oh no, he didn't. It was my idea."

Co.'s eyebrows crawled up his forehead. "Yes?"

Her courage suddenly failed her. "I'm sorry, Co.," she said humbly.

"That's better." Co. gave her a soothing pat. "We don't blame *you*, Muggles. You've been led astray. Now I suggest you stay here quietly among these venerable objects and think things over."

Muggles would have preferred to think in her own cozy cottage, but she didn't dare go against Co.'s orders, so she stared hard at the family tree and the painting or, according to Walter the Earl, at the painting and the family tree, until the daylight had quite gone.

When she left the museum at last, Etc. had already performed the ritual of striking fire to the reed-light. Muggles hurried past it on the far side to escape its fumes. The marketplace was empty except for herself and—

A sodden, muddy figure staggered from the Street Going to the River into the square. He wavered a few steps farther and then, with a little cry, fell into a heap and did not rise.

"Gummy!" Muggles flew across the cobblestones to the huddle of yellow cloak. "Gummy, is it really you?"

He gave a groan and rolled over to stare glassily at the burning reed.

"Etc. lit a little light," he mumbled.

"Etc. lit a little light,
And now we've got it every night.
It may burn orange as new quince jelly,
But let's admit it's rather smelly!"

"Hush," said Muggles, looking fearfully over her shoulder. "What happened to you? Where have you been?"

Gummy's eyes flickered shut and then open again. "Fell overboard. Coming home from mountains. Almost . . . didn't make it. . . . Been . . . keeping watch . . . last two nights. . . ."

"Did you— What did you—Gummy!" She gave him a little shake as his eyes began to close again.

"Pocket . . . right-hand pocket."

Quickly, Muggles searched first one pocket, then the other. "No, there's nothing. Gummy! What was it?"

Gummy gave a groan. "Must have fallen out . . . in the river. Just a . . . half-burned twig . . ."

"Half-burned twig?" cried Muggles. "But what—?"

"It . . . it blew off the mountain."

She stared at him.

"Brought it home to prove to Co. Doesn't matter . . . Wouldn't believe . . . anyway . . ."

Muggles half pulled, half carried Gummy inside her house.

After she had wrapped him in her comforter and given him some soup and two cups of strong hot tea, he promptly fell asleep, curled up on her bed.

Muggles stood looking down at his white, drawn face for a few minutes. *Not altogether undependable after all*, she thought. *It just depends on what you're depending on.*

Curley had a little door,
Its color was bright scarlet.
It blazoned forth both night and day,
By sun and moon and starlet.
Till one dark night . . .

—Wm., *Uncompleted Poem*

It was fully dark now except for Etc.'s reed-light. Muggles blew out the candle and huddled before her fire where she could keep watch on the distant Sunset Mountains through the window.

Like fish being handed from a fishing boat and counted, her worries flopped one by one into her mind: Curley Green's scarlet door . . . the mutterings against Walter the Earl . . . Co.'s visit to the museum . . . the secret of the treasures in the vault . . . the words of the Seventeenth Earl—"It is my belief that such a one will appear when he is needed for the safety of his people." And underneath all these nagging, torturing worries lay the biggest one of all, that she hardly dared look at— the fires on the mountains. Fires on the mountains! Things—people—out there spying down upon the valley. Trying to get in. Gummy said they couldn't come over the Sunset Mountains, but how could he be sure? They had got up the other side, hadn't they? And even if they couldn't come over the cliffs at that place, who was to say there weren't other spots, farther up the valley, open to them? Muggles shuddered.

A small, secret, furtive sound on the still night air brought her upright. Who would be in the marketplace at this hour? Forcing herself to stand up, she went to her door and softly opened it. There were no lights visible in any of the cottages, and the reed-light in the center of the marketplace had settled down to a soft glow, but there was enough illumination to make out a cloaked figure hurrying across the square. Muggles's eyes widened. It was certainly Geo., and he was carrying something. She stood and watched to see what he was about, while her wonderment changed to indignation. When Geo. at last returned across the marketplace, Muggles quietly closed her door and leaned against it, thinking hard. Then, her lips set in a determined line, she lit the candle and stole across the room to extract the things she needed from various heaps and piles. When all was in readiness, she swung her door open and set to work.

At last she was finished, and she stepped back with a pleased smile. It was even more glorious than she had expected. She put her materials carefully away where they belonged, and sat down before the fire again. And though she was trembling a bit at her daring, the corners of her mouth curved into a satisfied smile.

8

When something happens, something
else always happens.

—Muggles, *Maxims*

When the sun got up the next morning, Thatch had
already placed his ladder against Fooley Hall and
climbed up on the roof to start work. With his bundle
of dried reeds on his back, he crawled along, whis-
tling softly around the clove of garlic he always
sucked as a remedy against chills, and counting in
his head the number of gold pieces he would have
by the end of the week.

When he reached the chimney, he stood up to
survey the roofs still to be done in the new scalloped
fringe—one gold-bit for each. It was an encouraging
sight, and Thatch's heart swelled with happiness.
Roofs to the north of him, roofs to the west of him,
roofs to the . . . Perplexed, Thatch turned back to
scan the houses on the west side of the marketplace.
What was different about them this morning?
What—? He clutched the chimney in astonishment.

Curley Green's door was as green as the greenest door on the square!

"*Well!*" said Thatch, shifting the garlic from one cheek to the other. He swept his gaze round the marketplace, at the rows of shining white houses and uniform green doors. Then he clutched the chimney again, his eyes almost popping out of his head. Across the square from Curley Green's door glowed a splotch of bright color. Thatch blinked and blinked again. It was Muggles's house, and her door was painted a vivid orange!

"*Well!*" said Thatch, and gaped so broadly that his garlic fell out and rolled down the roof unheeded.

Other folk had more to say when they discovered the changes wrought during the night. Small groups clustered together on the cobbles to whisper and glance sidelong at the two doors, broke up, and reclustered to whisper some more. Somebody—no one knew who—started a rumor going that Geo. the Official Village Painter knew more about Curley Green's painted door than Curley Green herself. When this news circulated itself among the clusters, there was a sound like a gobble of fish snapping at green flies.

Reedy, the basketmaker's wife, was indignant. "Right or wrong," said she, "it's Curley Green's door, and Geo. has no business meddling with it behind her back."

Bun, the baker's wife, was more cautious. "But Geo. being a Period . . . Now, if it was somebody ordinary, like Dingle or Spill or Thatch, that did the painting, we should know at once it was wrong, but with Geo. being a Period . . . well, there's a difference, Reedy."

"That's right. There's a difference," Wove the Weaver agreed.

"Periods know what is right and what is wrong," said Dingle the Miller solemnly. "It has always been that way. Don't the Periods hold the high offices because of their wisdom?"

"Yes, yes!" everybody agreed.

The question settled, the clusters began to break up, but just then there was a new diversion. The door of Gummy's house opened, and Gummy stepped outside.

Instantly, every eye was riveted on him.

He set a pail down on his doorstone. With a carefree air, he produced a brush, dabbled it in the pail, cocked his head from side to side, and then, raising the dripping brush, he applied a broad stroke of yellow paint to his door.

On the west side of the square Walter the Earl

stepped out on his doorstone and methodically began to paint his own door bright blue.

The tense silence of the watching villagers broke into a concerted gasp.

"How do they dare!" cried Bun.

"The Periods will never stand for it!"

"Stand for what?" demanded Scot., the town clerk's wife. She and Eng., followed by Wm. and Geo., pushed their way through the excited cluster. "If it's poor simple Muggles and her door, you needn't concern yourselves . . ."

For answer, Fin Longtooth pointed first at Gummy's house, then at Walter the Earl's.

"Why, those—" Geo. started forward, his face aflame.

Wm. held on to him. "Ltd. said no more fuss," he warned.

"But they're cheating us of the Gammage Cup with every stroke!" Eng. cried shrilly.

The ordinary villagers, jolted by this new thought, began to grumble in indignation.

"Shouldn't be allowed, then," Fin Longtooth declared. "Now I remember when there was a bit of trouble over cutting down a family tree . . ."

"Of course, it's *their* doors," Reedy pointed out.

"But it's *our* village!" cried Bun.

"They shouldn't be allowed to spoil our village!"

Geo. suddenly turned and made off for the mayor's house.

Ignoring his audience, Gummy covered the last bit of his door with paint and stepped back to admire the effect. Then he took his pail and brush and himself inside. Walter the Earl had already disappeared behind his bright blue door.

Unaware of these happenings, Muggles was just getting up. The night's vigil had been long and unrewarding, for there were no fires to be seen on the mountains, and at dawn she had fished an old comforter from the under-the-table heap and made a cozy bed by the fire.

When she woke up, Gummy had gone, leaving on her table a scribble.

> "For picking me up
> And taking me in,
> For cheating the mice
> Of nibbling my chin—
> THANKS!
>
> "For the use of your bed
> And the soup and the tea,
> May you never regret
> What you've done for me.
> THANKS!"

"I hope I won't," Muggles murmured. She made herself a pot of watercress tea and three fish cakes and after restoring the old comforter to its proper place and otherwise making her house neat and tidy, she ventured forth. The brightness of her door as she swung it open made her wince. It was *very* orange by daylight. Still, nobody seemed to be bothering his head about it. She struck straight across the marketplace toward the museum.

A lot of villagers were clustered round the lamp-post where Geo. was putting up a hastily lettered sign. Muggles paused on the fringe of the crowd to read it.

Notis
First Spring Meeting
After Tee—Important

With three sharp raps of his tap hammer, Geo. nailed the notice securely to the post.

"And now," he crowed, stepping back, "we'll see about *Them!*"

9

You never can tell
From a Minnipin's hide
What color he is
Down deep inside.

—Gummy, *Scribbles*
(Collected Works)

There was no loitering over tea in Slipper-on-the-Water that afternoon. Fish cakes and watercress were downed in a hurry, dishes washed even more hurriedly, and then, snatching up their stools, the villagers made their way to the marketplace to talk in whispering groups until time for the meeting to begin.

Only Muggles remained inside her house. In one hand she held her ordinary brown sash, in the other, her orange. She would have to decide very soon . . .

There was a stir in the marketplace, and then the buzz of voices hushed. Ltd. had just emerged from the mayor's house and was walking in stately slowness across to the meetinghouse.

The brown or the orange . . . ?

Muggles peered out her window at the slowly moving throng following Ltd. Like a patch of sunset sky, Curley Green's scarlet cloak flamed at the doorway of the meetinghouse beside Mingy's patched green, and then was swallowed up. Muggles dropped one of the sashes on the floor and hurried out into the marketplace.

When Curley Green and Mingy slipped into the gloom of Fooley Hall, they placed their stools neatly in line with the others already there, and went up to the table to receive steaming mugs of watercress punch and biscuits. But when they went back to their places, the stools which had been beside theirs had pointedly been removed, while the row behind was filling up rapidly.

"Good," said Mingy, not looking at Curley Green. "Plenty of elbowroom. Hate being crowded. Folks crunching biscuits in your ear so you can't hear your own crunches."

Curley Green looked troubled. "Don't sit with me, Mingy," she said in a whisper.

"Sit where I please," Mingy snapped, and folded his arms.

Gummy and Walter the Earl threaded their way through the press of villagers a moment later and plumped their stools down beside Curley Green in the almost empty row.

"Good of you to save us a space," said Walter the Earl sardonically.

Muggles arrived breathless, her hastily tied orange sash askew. "Mind if I sit here?" she asked, putting her stool down next to Mingy. "Have a pepmint, do." And she passed a crumpled bag of sweets down the line.

Mingy took one with a scowl. "Why don't you be sensible and sit somewhere else?"

"Because this is where I belong," said Muggles with simple dignity.

In a few moments Fooley Hall was full and everybody had been helped to steaming mugs of punch and biscuits. But instead of the usual gay chatter of voices, a curious silence descended, broken only by a nervous whisper here and there.

There was no need to rap the wall for order, but Ltd. rapped anyway. The last whisper stopped abruptly.

"Good folk," said the mayor, "we have plans to make for receiving the three judges when they come. They may arrive any day now."

There was clapping of hands, and Ltd. smiled round at his audience. "Free paint has already been distributed to everybody, and I want to thank you for the promptness with which you have painted your cottages."

The clapping was more sporadic this time. Veiled glances were aimed in the direction of the sixth row of stools where gold and scarlet, yellow and orange intermingled, and there was an uneasy rattle of the money box.

"You have seen the excellent work already done by Thatch. He will continue until every roof in Slipper-on-the-Water has a scalloped fringe. All roofing will be paid for out of the money box."

Loud and prolonged applause greeted this statement. Mingy scowled and stood up.

"Then I must warn the assembled company that this raid on the money box will leave the village poor for the rest of the year!"

Co. leaped to his feet. "I should like to ask our money keeper just what he proposes to do with the village wealth. Stack it up in big piles and put it in the museum for everybody to look at?"

Mingy's face turned red. "I propose to spend it sensibly," he retorted. "Not on fancying up the village to win prizes. What good will scalloped roofs do if the dock suddenly caves in when the judges arrive? And then there's the sick fund. We need a sick fund to take care of folk when they have bad luck or can't work. What will the judges think if they see some of our villagers starving themselves for lack of a gold piece?"

A murmur of approval started up, but it was quickly quelled by Wm. "As to that," he cried, "I am *sick* of hearing about Mingy's *sick* fund! It's pure foolishness, as I can show in one moment. Is there anybody here who is starving to death?"

There were mutters of "No" and "Of course not," although Spill the Candlemaker and a few others stirred uncomfortably on their stools. Spill's candles were more costly to make than Etc.'s reed-lights, and he was feeling the pinch.

Bros. popped up to speak. "It's clear enough that Mingy doesn't *want* us to win the Gammage Cup—along with several others!" He darted a venomous look at the outcast row. "*I* say, let's get on with the meeting for the sake of the rest of us who do!"

"Very well," said Ltd. "The meeting is thrown open for suggestions as to what more may be done to our village that will help us to win the Gammage Cup."

Geo. sprang up. "Green doors!" he burst out. "Everybody should have a green door. It spoils the appearance of the village if folk are going to paint their doors any old color they please."

"And green cloaks!" his wife Eng. cried. "Proper, decent Minnipin green cloaks for everybody so we'll not feel ashamed!"

"Ahum, yes," said Ltd., "the matter of color . . ." He stroked his beard with nervous fingers. "I am going to make an appeal to certain members of our village." He fixed the row of gold and scarlet, yellow and orange, with a stern eye. "Now, then . . . there seems to be a difference of opinion about what color is proper to a Minnipin's door and a Minnipin's cloak."

"Don't forget Walter the Earl's sword!" cried Co.

"And the candy warriors Muggles made!" cried Scot.

"And what they're saying about the family tree!" This was from Geo. and Wm. together.

Ltd. held up his hand for silence. "We won't go into that for the moment. The question right now is: Shall we all have green doors and green cloaks, which are traditional with Minnipins, or . . . Walter the Earl, do you wish to address the meeting?"

Walter the Earl kept his hands folded over his ashplant and pushed himself to his feet.

"I painted my door blue because I objected to *someone's* sneaking out at night and painting Curley

Green's door without her consent or knowledge. I wear my gold-embroidered cloak because it suits me. My family was a family of warriors, and in the old days, long before they came to this valley, they wore the gold with pride. History—*fact* history, not Fool history—"

Co. gave an excited shout. "There! You see, he's insulting Fooley!"

"Fooley's name was properly The Fool while he lived," said Walter the Earl coldly. "I see no reason for changing it now."

There were cries of indignation over the hall. Several Periods jumped to their feet with fierce shouts. Ltd. banged hard on the wall.

"Gummy?"

With a flowing motion Gummy stood up.

"When the sun is shining on the trees,
Dappling the green with golden ease,
And spring is bursting in every part,
I must wear yellow o'er my heart."

He made a deep bow and sat down again. There was a heavy silence.

"Curley Green?" said Ltd. with a sigh.

She got up slowly and looked about at all the familiar faces in the hall. "I'm sorry," she said softly,

"I'm sorry that my door seems to have started all this trouble. I hadn't realized that it was so offensive to everybody. I even thought, but I suppose this is silly, that there were some folk who enjoyed looking at my door . . ."

Thatch suddenly straightened himself. "Well . . ." he began, but then his tongue got tangled up with the garlic clove in his mouth, and before he could get it popped back into his cheek, his voice was drowned out.

"Not likely," snorted Eng.

"An eyesore to the whole village," said Geo.

"Poor excuse!"

"More impudence!"

Ltd. made banging sounds and nodded to Muggles, who turned white and then pink with embarrassment as she wobbled to her feet.

"I don't know much about things," she faltered, "but—well, it seems to me—" She stopped short and looked round for rescue, but there was nobody to help her out. Then she caught Curley Green's eye, and Curley Green smiled at her. "What I mean is," she went on, "well, I don't think it's doors or cloaks or . . . or orange sashes. It's *us*. What I mean is, it's no matter what color we paint our doors or what kind of clothes we wear, we're . . . well, we're those colors inside us. Instead of being green inside, you see, like other folk. So I don't think maybe it would do any good if we just changed our outside color. We would still be . . . be orange or scarlet inside, and, well, we would do orange and scarlet things all the time, and everybody would still—"

"Really!" said Eng. "She *is* simple!"

"Yes, I know," Muggles agreed. "Everybody always says so. But what I really want to say is, wouldn't it be cheating if we changed our outsides just for the judges? I mean, it doesn't seem quite fair, does it?" She tried to think of something more to explain, but her brain was already dizzy from its exertion. She sat down.

"Good sense," Mingy said suddenly. "Most sense I've heard today. Me, I like green. Good sensible color. Doesn't show dirt. Don't have to wash it to pieces, waste soap and water. How would I like it if somebody came along and said I had to wear yellow now? Wouldn't do it. Don't know what color I am inside. Don't think I'm green, though. Probably a good sensible brown. Doesn't show the dirt. But whatever color it is, I'm not going to change it for all the judges in the Land Between the Mountains."

Villagers exchanged bewildered glances. One or two shuffled their feet as though they would rise and speak, but each waited for the other, and by that time the official village painter had the floor.

"I've never heard so much nonsense!" Geo. sputtered. "Ridiculous! All this chatter about folk being green inside, or orange, or scarlet—ridiculous, I say!"

"We've put up with them long enough!" Wm. cried. "Them and their blobs and scribbles and history. They—"

"They teach our children bad things!" interrupted Scot.

"And only yesterday," said Geo., "Co. caught them *tampering* with the museum!"

"Tampering with the *museum!*" somebody said in a shocked voice.

"That's right!" Geo. said triumphantly. "They will do anything. Anything!" He dropped his voice almost to a whisper. "Good folk, you know what happens to a gobble of fish when a lamprey enters the river. Unless it is found and cast out, the fish disappear, one by one." He paused, and everybody hung breathless on his words. "It is plain to see that we now have five lampreys in our village. Every minute that these lampreys spend with us from now on is a minute of *danger!*"

"Lampreys!" Fin Longtooth gasped, and turned white.

"Lampreys!" echoed the villagers, and those sitting near that row of bright color cringed away from it.

The town clerk now rose to his feet and faced the assemblage. "Am I right in thinking that all of you want the Gammage Cup to come to Slipper-on-the-Water?"

"Yes!" the villagers shouted with one accord.

"And am I right in believing that you trust the Periods, your own Periods in your own village, to do all they can to get it for you?"

"*Yes!*"

"Then," Co. intoned, "we must take action against these troublemakers, these . . . these *destroyers*." He paused for a deep breath. "They must be *outlawed!*"

For a second there was silence in the hall. Then came a horrified sucking-in of breath from the assembly. Not to live in a village securely surrounded by neighbors—a Minnipin could hardly even imagine such a thing. No one had ever before been outlawed. It was the worst of all punishments, written down in the law books but never used.

The dreadful word went whispering around the hall . . . outlawed . . . *outlawed* . . .

Ltd. rapped for order; he looked unhappy. "Now, my good people, we must think very carefully—"

"That won't be necessary!" Walter the Earl stood up, straight and proud in his gold-embroidered cloak. "We have no wish to set Minnipins at odds with their consciences. Nor do we intend to stand in the way of their winning the Gammage Cup. We are not lampreys, but neither are we flies to be swallowed by trout. And so tomorrow morning we shall take leave of this village to settle elsewhere. In short, *we* are outlawing Slipper-on-the-Water."

Walter the Earl turned, and without a backward glance stalked from the meetinghouse. Curley Green and Gummy followed close behind him. For a moment Muggles and Mingy looked at each other, and then, in the awful waiting silence, they too rose and walked out.

The money box remained behind on Mingy's stool.

10

No matter where There is, when
you arrive it becomes Here.

—Muggles, *Maxims*

"How much farther is it?" Muggles panted, resting
her paddle on the side of the heavily laden boat.

"Just around the bend," Gummy called over his
shoulder. "Keep paddling, or you'll go backward!"

It was late afternoon, and they were making their
way in five boats up the Little Trickle toward the
Sunset Mountains.

It had been a day of hard toil and sadness and
excitement, starting at sunup. When Muggles had
rolled out of her feather bed and started reaching
for her clothes, she hadn't remembered at first what
was to be done that day. Then, when it came to her,
she almost rolled back into bed to hide under the
comforter. Could this really be happening to her, or
was it all a bad dream? Bad dream, of course, she
decided optimistically. Unthinkable that she could

have got herself so mixed up with folk like Curley Green and Gummy and—

At that moment there was a tap on her door, and when Muggles opened it and found Reedy and Bun on her doorstone, she knew that it hadn't been just a bad dream after all.

"We've come to help you pack," Reedy said stiffly, looking everywhere but at Muggles.

"Thank you," Muggles faltered. "You shouldn't—"

"I know. That's exactly what Crambo said. 'Reedy,' he said, 'you shouldn't get mixed up with orange doors and swords and the like. No good will come of it,' he said. 'Fiddlesticks, Crambo,' I said, 'if you want them out of the village, then the quickest way to remove them is to help them pack up.' Crambo's cautious, he is, but even he saw the sense of that." Her quick eyes darted around the room from pile to pile. "My, what heaps of stuff you've got. You planning to take all of it?"

"N-no," Muggles said. "You can have anything you like after—after we've gone."

"Now, that's what I call sensible." Reedy gave several brisk nods. "Come on, Bun. Don't stand gaping. There's work to be done."

Muggles moved back before their advance and

sank onto the stool Mingy had mended for her. It was really happening, then. Well, she was resigned to it, she thought with a sigh. Let them do with her belongings what they would. But as Reedy vigorously attacked the first pile, she gave a little choked cry and turned her head away.

It had taken a long time. At first, in spite of Muggles's determination to let Reedy and Bun have their way with her treasures, there had been arguments—over the packet of glitter-stones ("What *use* are they?" demanded Reedy. "But they're so pretty," begged Muggles, "all winking fire. Besides, they've always been in my family, so I've heard."); over the pebbles with magic properties ("There is no such thing as magic," said Reedy. "How can you be sure?" wailed Muggles.)—but in the end, Muggles retreated into a numb silence while Reedy and Bun discarded her treasures with ruthless abandon. Even so, the take-along heap reached alarming proportions and would have had to be sorted all over again had not Gummy promised to pick up the remaining pieces when he returned on the fifth day to bring back the four boats lent to the outlaws by vote of the Council of Periods.

There was no sending-forth party as the heavily laden craft set off, though more than one villager suddenly found that he had business which took him close to the dock. Loaf the Baker discovered that he had accidentally mixed too large a batch of bread for the villagers' use, and thrust a basket full of loaves into Curley Green's hands. Dingle had unaccountably found himself with too much flour and pressed a heavy bag of it upon them, lest it grow buggy in his mill. Reedy contributed a quantity of fresh reed-butter and fish patties in payment for the articles bestowed upon her by Muggles, and Spill surreptitiously slipped a bundle of candles into Mingy's boat, giving no reason at all for making such a gift. But most of the villagers stayed away, and the Periods stayed even more away as the five boats cast off from the dock, with Gummy in the lead.

Muggles looked back just once, as they rounded the bend. The dock was empty already, except for Reedy, who lifted her arm in a halfhearted wave of farewell. Then the bend cut the village from their view. A few minutes later Gummy had turned his boat into the smaller waters of the Little Trickle.

There was no time nor breath for talking. The boats lay so heavy in the water that even Gummy, accustomed to paddling for long hours, was too winded to shout out the rhymes that gathered in his head. For hours they labored upstream under the lonely trailing willow trees, with only the sound of paddles

striking the water, the occasional soft plash of a curious trout, the whir of birds startled from their perches, and the soft eerie stirrings of small animals along the banks. Once, Muggles stopped paddling and looked wildly about at the strangeness closing in on her. What was she doing here in a boat, rushing off from the old comfortable sounds of slippers pattering on cobblestones, the busy bustle and rustle of the marketplace, the . . .

"Look out!" warned Curley Green from the boat behind her. "We're going to bump!"

Muggles seized her paddle and plunged it into the water with a splash. *What's done is finished*, she told herself sternly. *Put your nose ahead and your face will follow . . . You can't take a step without putting forth a foot . . . Look where you're going before you look back—* But that was just the trouble! She didn't know where she was going. None of them did, except Gummy. Up the Little Trickle to a stone house on a knoll, he had described it, but where

was that, really? Where was anywhere once you had left the village?

"Almost there," Gummy sang out, and bent stronger to his paddle. A moment later he pulled in beside a crude dock concealed by an immense willow tree. Scrambling out, he moored his craft to the trunk of the tree and turned to help Muggles out of her boat.

Grassy banks dotted with blue and yellow flowers led upward from the stream to a knoll where tall trees sheltered a stone cottage with a woven willow roof. To the left of the knoll, the Little Trickle wound on to its source in the Sunset Mountains, only the peaks of which were visible through a break in the trees. The sun was already disappearing behind the crags in a fire of red and gold. Fire . . . Muggles shivered and looked back to the little stone cottage on the knoll.

"Well?" said Gummy.

"It looks," said Muggles, "why, it looks like Somewhere!"

Then there was no time for more talk, for Curley Green's boat had to be docked, and Mingy's, and last of all, Walter the Earl's. It took dozens of trips to carry all their supplies and small pieces of furniture up to the stone house. There were comforters and clothes, pots and stools, boxes and barrels and dishes. There were also five suits of armor, five jeweled war cloaks, five shields, one battle flag, and five swords.

Mingy scratched his head when these things came out of Walter the Earl's boat. "Are we going to have a battle?"

"You never know," Walter the Earl said stiffly, and turned away to see if his box of ancient parchments had come to any harm.

Gummy's house was a haphazard collection of stones fetched from the rock outcropping at the northern base of the knoll and slapped together with river clay. Tiny as it was (there was scarcely room to swing a turtle), it had been two years a-building. But there was a chimney and a fireplace with a clay oven, and even some crude shelves to hold dishes. The roof of woven willow wands, Gummy announced proudly, scarcely leaked at all except on one side, and then only when it rained. He had never bothered to patch it after he discovered the convenience of having running water in the house.

"And I suppose you just lie under the leak and hold your mouth open when you're thirsty," said Curley Green. "Not me, thank you. I'll sleep on the other side of the room."

But as more and more of the outlaws' possessions came through the door, the little house shrank alarmingly, until there was scarcely room for all five to stand up in.

Mingy stared morosely at the mounting heap of stuff. "Just where *are* we going to sleep?"

"Outside," said Gummy cheerfully.

"Outside!" cried Muggles, and "Outside!" the others echoed. They stared at Gummy as though he had said they would make their beds in the Little Trickle.

"Outside," Gummy repeated with firmness. "It's a fine night, so why not? Animals sleep outside, don't they?"

"When Gammage first came to the valley," Walter the Earl said thoughtfully, "they must have slept in the open."

"Then we sleep under the stars until we get another house built," said Mingy with a determined nod. "Won't say I relish the idea, but I daresay there'll be lots of new ideas we won't take to just at first. Thing to do is be cheerful. Do the thing that has to be done. Don't look backward."

They spread their comforters and blankets under the trees, and then they sat cross-legged on the grass in the dying light and ate supper from the good things the villagers had tucked into the boats. The plash of the Little Trickle sounded faintly in their ears, and the tall trees waved overhead.

"Tastes good," said Muggles.

"Ummm."

They settled down to their munching with sighs of contentment.

"Picklick," Curley Green said suddenly.

"What!"

"Picklick." Curley Green swept her piece of bread in a wide arc. "I've just invented a new word. It's what we're having now, a picklick. We pick around for what we want to eat, and then we lick our fingers."

Gummy, his mouth full, bobbed his head vigorously. "Thad's good." He chewed hard, swallowed, took another bite, and then talked around it:

> "Picklick in woods,
> Taste cool green air,
> Hear splash of brook,
> Feel spiders in hair.

> "Picklick in meadow,
> Watch butterflies flutter,

See sun on the grass,
Taste ants in the butter!"

By the time the first stars had appeared, the five outlaws were rolled into their comforters under the trees, listening to the soft night noises. A big white moon appeared over the Sunrise Mountains and sailed serenely through fluffs of white cloud.

"Good night and good dreams," Muggles murmured sleepily.

"Good dreams, everybody . . ."

"Good night . . ."

"Good dreams . . ."

"Queer thing," said Curley Green. "I don't remember ever really *looking* at stars before. They're kind of comforting . . ."

"Ummmm . . ."

Sometime during the night, Muggles woke up, bewildered. Where was she? What was she doing on the ground instead of being in her own little house snugged into her own little bed? Then she saw the moon drifting high overhead, and remembered. Propping her head on one elbow, she looked around at the others. They were all peacefully asleep. It was an eerie feeling, waking up all alone in the night . . . She rolled over to look at the Sunset

Mountains looming so close in the west. A smoky mist hung over them, but there were no fires to be seen. *They've gone away*, she thought sleepily. *The Mushrooms, or whatever they are, have given up and gone off.*

With a yawn, Muggles settled herself down in her warm comforter and went back to sleep.

11

Drive them, kick them,
Make them work;
Take away the pat-cakes
From those who shirk.

Groan, groan, moan, and sigh.

Humor them, coax them,
But make them slave;
Drive them to toil
Till they fall in the grave.

Groan, moan, sigh, good-bye.

—Gummy, *Scribbles*
(Collected Works)

The next three days swirled by in a dizzy round of
hard work that left no time for idle regrets over the
easy life they had left behind them. At first they
went about their tasks in a helter-skelter fashion so
that nothing they started ever seemed to get quite

finished. A second house *must* be built; watercress beds *must* be planted. Edible roots and herbs *must* be found; some way of milling the reeds into flour *must* be discovered. And all these things *must* be done at once, along with the ordinary chores of fishing, cooking, washing of clothes.

"It fairly makes your head spin," said Muggles wearily at sundown of that first day. They had just eaten, for in the hustle of events, nobody remembered that there was no Staggers the Supplys Keeper here to turn to, and Gummy and Walter the Earl had had to set forth with fishing rods late in the day while the others grubbed in the woods for the sweet root of the brown-sticker plant.

"What we need is more order in our work," Muggles went on. "We're going about it so untidily. I do dislike untidiness."

"I daresay you're right," said Gummy, stretching out on the grass with a tremendous yawn, "but work's not the sort of thing you can pile up in neat little heaps. In fact, I don't think work is my sort of thing at all." He rolled over and pulled his toil-stained yellow cloak around him. "I'm so tired that nothing even rhymes in my head." His voice drifted off into nothing.

Curley Green roused him enough to make him stumble off to bed, and all the outlaws were soon under their comforters, but their "Good nights" and "Good dreams" sounded dispirited.

Only Muggles remained awake, disturbed by the day's toil just past. Though the others tackled a new job cheerfully enough, starting out at top speed, they couldn't seem to stay at it for very long. More and more frequently they paused to talk or gaze at the sky or walk down to the Little Trickle for a drink of fresh water, until work became just an interval between idleness instead of the other way around. Muggles set a good example by toiling on with whatever task was at hand, but it was impossible to make an impression on folk who just weren't there to watch. Even Mingy, who was steadier than the others, was not as reliable as Muggles could wish. Instead of going directly to the rock outcropping at the northern base of the knoll and carrying a load of stones directly back to the top, he was disposed to linger in the quarry, examining the rock formation, exclaiming over curiously shaped stones. By midday, when they sat down to a scratch dinner, there was only a pitifully small mound of stones at the site of the new house. But nobody save Muggles appeared to be anything but pleased with what they had wrought.

Then, after dinner and a nap, Mingy announced his idea of making a cart from two barrel tops and a basket so that they could haul the stones in it instead of over their shoulders. Immediately everybody clamored to help mount the barrel tops on an axle of stout ash which had previously been a broken paddle. But when they came to build the framework that would hold the basket between the two wheels, it was discovered that they would have to cut wood, and while Muggles had brought with her an old axhead, it had no handle. Just as enthusiastically as they had plunged into the making of the cart, they now cast it aside and rushed off to rummage on the forest floor for a suitable stick that would serve as a temporary handle so that they could then use the ax to make a proper handle for itself. When suppertime caught up with them, though they ached in every joint, they had no more to show for their hard day's toil than one passable ax, the head of which flew off at every fourth stroke, two wheels on an axle, and a small pile of stones.

At this rate, Muggles thought, winter will be upon us with no house built, no food supplies stored, and all of us miserable and worn out and bickering with each other . . . How had those first Minnipin settlers managed when they came to the Land Between the Mountains with their two-wheeled carts? Was there a leader in each village to tell folk what to do next, or had they flopped aimlessly about like hooked fish in a boat? *We've got to stop flopping*, Muggles said to the early stars winking in the sky. There was the fishing . . . the watercress beds . . . a garden . . . mill . . . storage cellar . . . the new house . . . Plans and schemes began to froth in her head like water over rapids.

On that second morning Muggles was up before the sun. When the others rolled their aching limbs out of their comforters, they were greeted by the spicy scent of herb tea and the teasing warm aroma of pat-cakes drifting from Gummy's stone house. After a quick wash in the chill waters of the Little Trickle, they appeared at the door to find the house glistening with cleanliness. The heaps of stuff they had brought from the village and dumped willy-nilly on the floor were carefully sorted and put away on shelves and in barrels and baskets.

"There is nothing tidier than a good neat pile," Muggles explained, "as long as there's just one person in the house. But it won't do for five, I can see that. So we'll just have to muddle along with everything hidden away until we each have a house of our own."

After they had eaten all the pat-cakes and drunk the herb tea, Gummy leaned back and patted his stomach. "Out with it, Muggles," he said with a resigned sigh. "A mole in a pitch-black tunnel could see you're bursting with plans for us. What do we have to do to pay for that breakfast?"

"You don't *have* to do anything," Muggles said slowly, "but if you *want* to do something, well, I've had sort of an idea about things, if you'd like to hear. And if—"

"Lot of if-ing," Mingy rumbled. "Best just speak out before we all get hungry again."

Walter the Earl regretfully put aside the parchment he had picked up after disposing of his last pat-cake. "I'm listening."

"And so am I," said Curley Green. She cast a wistful look at her paintbox on the shelf, but took down Muggles's mending box instead and threaded a bone needle with a length of yellow reed-silk. "Hand me your cloak, Gummy. There's a rip in it."

From one of the round squat barrels Muggles drew forth an enormous net, a smaller one of finest mesh, and two scoops. These she laid out on the floor.

"It seems to me," she said diffidently, "it seems to me we'll waste too much time if we have to stop work every day to fish for our dinners. Now, my idea is this. Gummy and Walter the Earl can stake the big net beside the dock with the sides well above the water so that fish can't swim out of it. Then they use the two scoops to catch enough trout for several days' supply, which they will put inside the net to swim around until we need them. The fine mesh is for eggs, which you must also look for. You can anchor the little net inside the big one, and as the eggs hatch and the fish grow larger, we will empty them into the big net to make room for more eggs. By wintertime, when fishing is difficult, we will no longer have to fish at all. It will be like a garden, only a fish garden, of course."

For a moment there was startled silence, and then the others burst out in loud exclamations of praise.

"But let's all help!" begged Curley Green. "I'd like to collect the eggs."

"You must be quiet and listen," said Walter the Earl. "Muggles is talking the most sense I have ever heard. And *there* is a fact." He turned his keen eyes back on her. "What else needs to be done, Muggles?"

"Well, while you and Gummy are making the fish garden," Muggles went on, blushing pink with pleasure, "Mingy could finish his cart for hauling rocks, and Curley Green might mark out the lines for the walls of the new house. I thought I would make a mill and grind a supply of flour—it will have to be green flour until we can make a harvest next season, but flour we must have."

"But how can you make a mill?" Curley Green asked, biting a thread.

"Oh, it won't be much of one—not like Dingle the Miller's, though later I don't see why we can't have a regular waterwheel to grind for us—but I saw a hollowed-out rock yesterday down in the quarry. All I have to do is find a longish thin stone with a rounded end that will fit into the hollow bit, and I'll grind the reed into flour with that."

"I'll help you grind," offered Mingy. "That's a hard task."

"No." Muggles's voice was firm. "There are too many things that want doing right away if we are going to make ourselves a good life on this knoll. After we've finished the new house, we must dig a storage cellar to keep roots over the winter, and we ought to have a garden right here where it will be convenient in wet weather. Then I saw some water-cress in a tiny stream that flows into the Little Trickle—that was on our way here from Slipper-on-the-Water—and though it's too far to go each time we need watercress, we can make a trip there to gather the roots and transplant them in the Little Trickle close to the knoll. Then, after we're sure of our food supply, we'll want to make furniture for the new house, and invent a way of getting water up the knoll and—"

"I can see that it's going to be a long summer," Gummy said wryly.

Curley Green cast another wistful look at her paintbox on the shelf. "Do you think, Muggles . . . that is . . . will there be *any* time at all for making blobs and scribbles and things like that?"

"And the old mines in the mountain," Walter the Earl added. "I want to see those for myself soon."

Muggles nodded vigorously. "Of course. Just as soon as we've got the new house finished, we'll only need to work in the mornings at the other things. But just now—"

"Just now," Walter the Earl broke in, "it seems we've got a fish garden to make, so let's be about it. Come on, Gummy." He scrambled to his feet and threw his worn cloak back over his shoulders. "Muggles, my compliments," he said gravely with a deep bow, and planting his hat firmly on his head, he strode to the door. Gummy made an even deeper bow. "At your service, taskmaster." He grinned impudently and followed Walter the Earl.

By midmorning the fish garden was complete, the cart was ready, the lines for the new house were marked out and some of the stones laid, and a supply of green flour was spread out to dry. At midday there were enough stones and wet clay delivered to the top of the knoll to make an earnest start on the house. Muggles called a halt to the work when the sun was directly overhead, and they sat down to a big dinner of fish scooped from the new fish garden and broiled over the fire, a pot of creamy milkroot spiced with fresh wild onion, and pepmint pudding, invented by Muggles on the spur of the moment.

"A-a-ah," Gummy sighed, stretching himself out on the grass with his knees cocked. "Just the sort of afternoon for lying under one's hat and listening to the buzz of the bees. Don't forget to wake me up for tea." And he carefully tilted his peaked hat over his face and lowered his knees until he was flat out.

Muggles looked fixedly at him and then at the others.

"Just a *teeny* little rest?" Curley Green pleaded. "Then I promise I'll get Gummy up. I'll pour water in his ears."

Gummy gave an imitation snore and clapped his hands over the sides of his head.

"All right," Muggles said and added craftily, "I'll brew a pot of sassafras tea and call you when it's ready."

"You ought to nap, too," Mingy murmured sleepily.

The peaked hat over Gummy's face bobbled with his muffled words. "Don't be odd. How can she think up more bone-breaking tasks for us if she naps?"

But they'll be glad they worked so hard when it's all done, Muggles thought as she busied herself over the fire in Gummy's house. The urge to close her eyes was almost overpowering, but she fought off sleep by mixing a batch of biscuits with some of the flour Dingle had given them and sprinkling the tops with poppy seed from her precious store.

Refreshed by the steaming sassafras tea, even Gummy threw himself into work with a will once more, and all afternoon the outlaws hauled stones from the quarry and set them in place with the plaster of clay until the walls were waist-high. When Gummy scanned the sky and sniffed the air and pronounced rain for that night, Muggles and Curley Green hurried into the woods to dig milkroot and wild-pea and crimson ground-berry plants, while Walter the Earl turned over the soil at one edge of the knoll for the transplants. The rain spattered down just as they got the last wildpea plant set into the garden, and they ran for the shelter of the house, joined by Mingy and Gummy, who had just panted up the side of the knoll with a last cartload of rock.

There was no sleeping out under the tree that night, so after supper they rolled themselves into their comforters on the floor. But after everybody had wished everybody else good dreams, Mingy said suddenly, "Stuffy, isn't it? Tomorrow I'll build a shelter out from that biggest tree. Roof on poles. Sleep outside, wet or fine. Plenty of fresh air, but no rain in the face. What do you think, Muggles?"

And Muggles, who as far back as she could remember had never been consulted over the simplest matter, gravely (and sleepily) gave her consent.

The third day dawned bright and crisp. All morning long, while Mingy constructed the sleeping shelter of thickly laced twigs and branches, the other outlaws, with occasional coaxings and proddings from Muggles, lugged stones up the knoll in the two-wheeled cart and cemented them into place with the river clay. Curley Green disappeared for a long interval, and when she reappeared looking flushed and secretive, Muggles wondered if she had sneaked off to paint a blob, but she pretended not to notice the long absence. *Perhaps*, thought Muggles, *perhaps she feels that I am driving her and the others too hard. Perhaps she feels that I have no right, and I haven't really, except that somebody has to see that the work is done. All the same*, she concluded wisely, *possibly it would be a good idea to think up something different from carrying rocks for the rest of the day.*

At midday, then, as they sat down to stuffed roast trout with tarragon sauce, she suggested an expedition by boat down the Little Trickle to the tiny stream where she had seen the watercress growing, and was met with four beaming faces and a muffled whoop from Gummy.

The expedition was a great success. They took all five boats ("A waste not to, for we'll have only one very soon," said Mingy.) and when they reached the stream, they pulled in to the bank and walked along it until they came to where the watercress grew thickest. Leaving their woven slippers on the grass, they waded and splashed among the tender green plants, extracting a root here and a root there, until the baskets they had brought were heaped with cool fresh watercress. Curley Green's sharp eyes spotted berry bushes growing in a sunlit glade, but it was too early for berries. "We'll come back when they are ripe," said Muggles. "I'll make jam for the winter." Then Mingy found honey in a hollow tree, and several stings later had extracted a goodly supply.

"Now this is *my* idea of work," said Gummy, laying himself out on a patch of grass to dry. "You can't make rhymes when you're carrying rocks. All the rocks get in your head and rumble around." He began to sing:

"We're outlaws five,
And bold and free;
We've built our house
Beneath a tree,
Above the Trickle's foam.

"We wander far
And wander wide,
But we always know
Deep down inside
The Kno-oll is our home.

"Jingle, tingle, ring-a-ling-ling,
Hear the song that the outlaws sing!"

The sun was still high in the sky when Muggles cajoled them back to the boats with a promise of fresh watercress for tea.

"Too bad we didn't bring the tea along *with* us," said Curley Green.

"Bring it with us!" Muggles exclaimed in shocked surprise. "Why, nobody ever—" she stopped and added dubiously, "Well, I suppose it *could* be done . . ."

"Let's do it tomorrow, then," said Walter the Earl. "I have in mind a trip to those old mines in the mountain. What do you think, Muggles? If we finish the walls of the new house, of course," he added hastily.

Muggles felt a sudden chill race up her back. The mountain! She had almost forgotten about the mountain. "Why, of course," she said slowly. "I . . . I don't see why not."

"I'm shoving off!" Gummy called from his boat, and he began his song:

> "We're outlaws five,
> And bold and free—"

The others joined in as they paddled up the Little Trickle against the current.

Still singing lustily, they rounded the last bend and came in sight of the knoll rising from the bank of the stream. Muggles felt her heart warm when she saw, rising beside Gummy's cottage, the walls of the new stone house. *By midday tomorrow*, she thought, *those spaces left in the sides will really be windows. The chimney still has to be built, but we'll get a roof on first. Woven willow, that's easiest, but next year perhaps we'll thatch. And it's ours, it belongs to us*, she told herself exultantly. *We didn't call in Clay the Plasterer and pay him gold pieces to build it for us . . .*

But in the middle of her exultation, a picture of

the marketplace of Slipper-on-the-Water flashed clear and sharp upon her mind, and she felt a sudden longing to be back in the village once again. The next instant she had beaten down this treacherous emotion, but it remained only just submerged in her mind, ready to leap out at an unwary moment.

Guiltily, she watched the others docking their boats. They were laughing and talking as though they hadn't a care in the world. Even Mingy's face had taken on new crinkles, and the old frowning ones seemed smoothed out. *I'm much happier here*, Muggles told herself firmly. And it was true. Still— She looked off up the Little Trickle to the piece of the Sunset Mountains visible through the trees, and her thoughts veered to the fires she had seen—how many mornings ago? There had been no time to wonder or worry about fires since they had got to the knoll. But tomorrow they were going—

"I say, Muggles," Curley Green called from the dock, "can't we wait till morning to plant the water-cress?"

Muggles jerked herself out of her uneasy reverie and paddled briskly toward the dock. "We must do it now while the roots are fresh," she said in the firm tone she had learned to use whenever work was to be done. "There is a good shallow spot just up-stream. We'll do all our bathing and washing of clothes *below* the dock so as not to dirty the fish garden."

Transplanting watercress proved to be a wet and muddy job, but at last the rootlets were all in, and the five outlaws trudged up the knoll to have tea. But the day's work was not yet over. The woodpile had to be replenished, and clothes must be washed. On this last point Muggles was adamant.

"We must not let ourselves become careless and wild," she said. "I've thought it all out. You have to be twice as neat and clean and tidy in the wilds just to stay civilized at all. So you must change clothes now, and I'll rub the dirt out of them on that nice big rock below the dock."

Mingy grumbled a good deal, complaining that clothes weren't really comfortable until they got somewhat stuck to the body, but in the end Muggles had her way. Gummy and Walter the Earl reluctantly went tramping off with the ax to cut up fallen branches for firewood, and in a few minutes Muggles was staggering down to the Little Trickle with a bundle of dirty clothes bigger than she. Curley Green's and Mingy's offers to help had been so halfhearted that she had refused them, though now she wished they had insisted upon coming. It would take hours of scrubbing and rinsing to get the soil out of all these things. However, it had been her idea to keep everybody clean, and clean they would be. *I must expect to do more than my share at first*, she thought. *They still haven't an idea of what it means to really work.*

Kneeling on the bank, she dipped the garments in the fast-flowing stream, rubbed them with soap, and began slapping them against the big flat rock. Soap. That was another thing. They would have to make soap before their present supply ran out. Wood ash and fat, they would need, and to get fat they would have to trap good fatty animals. Not a pleasant thing to do, not nearly as pleasant as calling at Sud the Soapmaker's, but then Sud got his fat from animals, so it amounted to the same thing in the end. Muggles scrubbed vigorously at Mingy's stained shirt and dipped it in the rushing stream.

Clothes, she thought suddenly. *When our clothes wear out, we'll have to make new ones.* She sat back on her heels to contemplate this new task. To make clothes, they must weave cloth; to weave cloth, they needed thread; to get thread, they must first spin it; and to spin it, they would need a spinning wheel. Muggles gave a little gasp. They didn't *have* a spinning wheel. For a moment the enormity of work which faced them in every direction almost overcame her then and there.

Just as the current was about to claim Mingy's

shirt for its own, Muggles came to herself and snatched it back. *There you go*, she scolded, *fussing about how we are going to make clothes and then almost losing a precious shirt while you worry needlessly about the future. As we don't have a spinning wheel, Mingy will just have to invent one, that's all. And spinning will give us something to do when the bad weather comes. Mingy must make a loom, as well. Then, while one spins the reed fibers, somebody else can be weaving the thread into cloth. We can take turns . . .* There sprang into her mind a picture of Walter the Earl solemnly manipulating warp and weft, his plumes a-nod with the effort, and she laughed along with the gurgle and splash of the merry Little Trickle.

All the same, she walked up the grassy slope with discouragement in each tired footstep, the great bundle of clean clothes clasped wetly to her front. There was no sign of the others as she stretched the garments to dry on the grass and pegged them tightly to roots, though from Gummy's house she could hear low murmurings interspersed with hushed laughter. At last the task was finished, and she sat back to survey her handiwork. Kneeling there on the grass in the darkening afternoon with only that low murmur to break the quiet—a murmur that seemed to shut her out—Muggles suddenly felt an infinite loneliness flooding over her. *I don't belong here*, she thought with despair. *Those others, even Mingy, are like crickets in the sun, while I am a miserable dull ant plodding along about my dull little business . . .* After a while she got up and with lagging feet walked heavily toward the door of Gummy's house.

There was a scramble inside, an urgent whisper, a muttered exclamation, and as she appeared in the open doorway, complete silence.

The other four outlaws were standing in the center of the room, their faces wreathed in smiles, and in their hands, stretched out so that she could see the beautiful billowing extent of it, was a glorious sun-orange cloak. Around the collar and down the two lapels, winking their fires of red and blue and green, were sewed the hundreds of glitter-stones that had always been in Muggles's family and that Reedy had tried to throw away.

Muggles looked from one face to another and then back at the wonderful cloak. The realization that here was the reason Curley Green had been slipping away from work swept all the loneliness right out of her.

"For . . . for *me?*" she faltered.

Walter the Earl nodded. "Of course, it's your own material and your own glitter-stones, but Curley

Green said you would never stop working long enough to sew it for yourself—"

"So we just sewed it for you," said Mingy. "Curley Green did most, but we helped finish it—all that time you were washing the comfort out of our clothes."

"And I may have had some hitches," said Gummy proudly, "but *I've* sewed the biggest stitches!"

12

A turtle should take fright
at the sound of a boiling pot.

—Muggles, *Maxims*

By the next morning the outlaws had their second wind (Gummy said it was his fourth or fifth), and the walls of the new house grew so high that the builders had to stand on piled-up barrels and chests to lay the stones. When the last stone was plastered into place, Walter the Earl was so carried away with the accomplishment that he began to dig a storage cellar between the two houses, being, as he pointed out, something of an expert on digging.

After their noonday dinner and a short nap, they set off upstream in the boats. ("Last time we can all ride at once," Mingy pointed out. "After tomorrow there will be only Gummy's boat, and we can't all squeeze into that." "We'll build a new one," said Muggles confidently. The others groaned in chorus.) But soon the Little Trickle narrowed, and the water became too shallow and fast to take the boats any farther. They had to tie them to trees along the stream's edge and proceed on foot, lugging the heavy picklick baskets with them. ("Easier to carry if the picklicks were inside us instead of in the baskets," Gummy suggested.) Walter the Earl had left his ashplant behind and brought one of the swords. He had fashioned a sling to carry it at his side, and it swung there at a rakish angle, thrusting out at his gold-embroidered cloak as he strode along.

After a while the trees began to thin out, and the soil became rocky, hurting their feet through their woven slippers. As they got closer to the base of the mountain, the sound of the burbling Little Trickle was overlaid by the deeper roar and splash of the waterfall tumbling down the side of the cliff, and now they occasionally saw bright glints in the streambed. Kicking off her slippers, Curley Green waded into the foaming water and retrieved a nugget large as an acorn, which she handed to Mingy.

"Gold," he said, turning it distastefully this way and that. He raised his arm to hurl it back into the Little Trickle, but Curley Green stopped him.

"It's naught but trouble, gold is," Mingy protested. "We've finished with money boxes and the like."

"But think what glorious things we can make with it," Curley Green said. "Doorknobs and dishes . . ."

"Cloth of gold," added Walter the Earl. "There was something in one of the ancient parchments about the making of gold thread. I wonder . . ." He fingered his cloak, which had grown even shabbier in the four days they had been gone from Slipper-on-the-Water. "This is the last of the three cloaks which belonged to my family, and it is threadbare. Muggles, do you think you could make gold thread?"

"If it's been done before, we can do it again," Muggles said with more certainty than she felt. How did one spin a thread out of a piece of hard metal? "We'll do it," she repeated, "just as soon as the roof is on the house and Mingy has made us a spinning wheel." You would probably have to melt the gold over a very hot fire. ". . . and a kiln," she added.

"We've arrived," said Gummy, stopping short. They had just rounded a great rock, and the mountain sloped up behind it, at first gently and then in a steep ascent to the sheer crags on top. To the left a slim waterfall cascaded like a long white veil and foamed into the shallow bed of the Little Trickle.

"It's—it's—" Muggles stammered, straining her neck to see the top. "Are you sure it won't tumble down on us?"

"Hasn't yet," answered Gummy. "And see, there
are the old mine entrances." He pointed to the gaping black openings in the rock-strewn slope. "I've
been in two or three of them—not very *far* in. It
gets lonely when you're by yourself."

They climbed up to the nearest opening and
ventured inside, into deepest gloom. That was far
enough for Muggles, but Gummy struck a light to a
bit of candle he had brought, and plunged ahead

into the blackness. Muggles started to back out into the sunshine, to let the others pass her if they wanted, but the space was so cramped that she only backed into Walter the Earl.

"Go on," he whispered hollowly. "We're following."

Muggles hesitated, dreading to be engulfed by that blackness, but the small gleam of Gummy's candle was bobbing farther and farther away, and there seemed nothing to do but follow. Fearfully, Muggles started forward, clutching her cloak around her to keep from brushing against the chill damp stone of the narrow passage. What slithery creatures might live here she dared not think, and she started at every scuttering sound, real or imagined. Ahead, the candle stopped its bobbing. She hurried faster to come up with Gummy, but when she reached him with the others close on her echoing heels, he merely grunted and started on again.

The tunnel sloped gently downward for a time and then leveled off, but Muggles was hardly conscious of anything as she stumbled along over the uneven floor, save that if she ever got out of this terrible place, she would never, never set foot in it again. Once she looked back at the others, but the feeble light of the candle cast large wavering shadows on the walls and ceiling behind them, like hulking monsters ready to spring, and she looked back no more.

When they had walked until Muggles thought they must surely be almost at the other side of the mountain, Gummy stopped so abruptly that she crashed into him. The candle flew from his fingers and sputtered out on the floor of the passage.

"Oh!" gasped Muggles, and the walls mocked her: *Oh . . . oh . . . oh . . .*

With a muffled exclamation Gummy dropped to his knees and began scrabbling about to find the bit of candle while the others waited in shivering, black silence. It was terrifying to have your eyes wide open and be able to see nothing . . . nothing . . . just the terrifying blackness pressing against your eyeballs. Gummy's searching became more frantic, and then at last the echoes picked up his gasp of relief as his fingers closed over the precious bit of wax. In a moment he had fumbled out his tinderbox and relit the candle. The darkness sprang back. Muggles discovered that she was clutching Walter the Earl's arm. Reluctantly, she let go her hold.

"Sorry," Gummy said sheepishly. "I thought I heard something."

Heard something . . . heard something . . . heard something, repeated the echoes.

They had come to a widening of the tunnel such

as they had passed before, but this one was almost the size of a small room, and indeed, in the flickering candlelight, several rotting old crates at one side looked like two chairs and a table.

"Cozy," said Curley Green. "We should have brought our baskets with us and had tea here."

Tea here . . . tea here . . . tea here, ran the echoes around them until they sounded like the titters of giggling imps.

"Let's go back," said Muggles with a shudder.

Go back . . . go back . . . go back . . .

"Yes," said Walter the Earl, who had poked at the rotting crates, only to see them crumble into dust at his feet. "I've had enough."

Enough . . . enough . . . enough, echoed the eerie voices.

Gummy passed the candle back to Mingy, who was at the end of the procession, and they turned to follow him upward out of the tunnel. But Gummy halted suddenly and clutched at Muggles's arm.

"Did you hear that?" he whispered.

Hear that . . . hear that . . . hear that . . .

They all stood perfectly still until the whispering echo had died away, and then they heard the sound.

Tap-tap-tap-tap. *Tap*-tap-tap-tap. *Tap*-tap-tap-tap.

Walter the Earl drew his sword from its sling.

Tap-tap-tap-tap . . . *Tap*-tap-tap-tap . . . *Tap*-
tap-tap-tap . . . It was like ten thousand fingernails
tapping on ten thousand tables, or myriads of raindrops beating on a rock wall. It wasn't a comforting
sound to hear in an abandoned gold mine in the
middle of a mountain with only a candle to light the
way.

Curley Green gasped. "Look at the sword!"

The sword . . . the sword . . . the sword . . .

Walter the Earl stared down at the blade and
almost dropped it. Where it had been black and
ugly before, now it glowed faintly with an inner
radiance.

"The secret!" Walter the Earl scarcely breathed
the words.

Secret . . . secret . . . secret, ran the whisper
around them and back and forth between the walls.

"Listen." Muggles put up a shaking hand. "The
tapping has stopped."

They strained their ears, but Muggles was right.
There was no further sound to be heard. And then
they looked back at the sword. The glow was gone,
and the blade was black and ugly as before.

"Let's get out of here," Mingy whispered.

Out of here . . . out of here . . . out of here . . .

The way back seemed endless. They stopped
once or twice to listen for the tapping sound, but

they didn't hear it again. Neither did the sword glow again. By the time they emerged from the gloom into the bright sunshine and the comforting sound of the cascade, they had begun to doubt their eyes and ears.

"It was the way the candle shone on the blade," Curley Green said.

Gummy nodded. "And the tapping was probably just dripping water. An underground spring, or something of the sort."

"Whatever it was, I didn't like it," Muggles declared. "It's no wonder Minnipins gave up mining!"

Walter the Earl said nothing, but he was frowning thoughtfully up at the rock face of the cliff towering above them.

"Let's eat," said Mingy.

They spread their picklick on top of the great rock near the mountain. Eating hungrily, they talked little. Each one kept glancing at the mine entrance. Afterward they searched along the Little Trickle for more gold nuggets and found enough to fill one of the small baskets. Then the daylight was nearly gone, and they had to hurry along homeward, but not without frequent looks behind them at the misty Sunset Mountains.

"It was only water dripping," Curley Green said

after a while. "It was the echo that made us imagine things."

"Of course," Muggles agreed. "But if it was water, why didn't it go on dripping?" *Don't be silly,* she scolded herself. *What does anybody know about old mines anyway? Maybe they always tap like that.*

They reached their knoll before it was quite dark. It had been a long day, and they were tired, so after a scanty supper they quickly snugged into their comforters under the shelter.

But before Muggles went off to sleep, she thought about the way the sword had gleamed in the tunnel. For it *had* gleamed. She was as sure of that as she was that her name was Muggles.

13

Welcum Gummy,
Welcum Muggles.
Don't tell us
About your struggles.

Good-bye Muggles,
Good-bye Gummy.
Take back home
Your empty tummy.

—Gummy, *Scribbles*
(Collected Works)

Soon after sunrise the next morning, Gummy and Muggles set off down the Little Trickle with the four boats in tow.

Muggles felt a pang of disloyalty. True, she had to get the rest of her belongings from Reedy, but Gummy could have done that just as well. Her real reason for going was . . . that she just couldn't stay away. She longed to feel the pat-pat of her slippers on cobblestones. With a sigh she smoothed the folds of her new bright-orange cloak and almost, but not quite, wished that she was wearing her old green. The glitter-stones winked and glimmered at her as the boat slid from shade into sunlight and back to shade again.

> "Birds are chirping,
> Fish are slurping,"

said Gummy dreamily. He paused and then added,

> "Down the Trickle,
> Where the fickle
> Morning breezes
> Come to tease us.

"Not very good," he said. "I think my rhyming needs new priming."

"Yes," Muggles agreed absently. She twisted around to look at the Sunset Mountains behind her. They loomed craggy and cold—and lifeless.

> "The birds are twittering,
> And squirrels chittering,
> As we go flittering
> Down the brook.

> "The dew is glittering,
> Grasshoppers spittering,
> And trout are frittering
> In search of a hook."

"That's not much better," said Gummy critically, "and it's the wrong season for grasshoppers. Some mornings I just can't get started." He looked over his shoulder at Muggles. "If I were you, I should stop worrying about the mountain, you know. The time to worry is when you know what you're up against, and then there isn't time to worry." He began to whistle.

The dock at Slipper-on-the-Water was empty when they landed, but it had been newly repaired and painted.

"No 'Welcum' banners for *us*," said Gummy. "Ah, well . . . lend us a hand here, Muggles." He started hauling in the string of boats they had towed, but Muggles didn't lend a hand. She was staring in bewilderment up the Street Going to the River.

"Now, what makes it look so different?" she asked with a frown.

"What looks different?" Gummy grunted, tugging at the boats.

"Why, it's the trees—the family trees! Oh, Gummy!" she wailed. "The family trees are all queer!"

Gummy hitched the first boat to its post before turning around. Then he stood, thunderstruck at the sight. Up the street the trees marched in a precise line, one to each house as was the custom, but instead of the haphazard pattern of leafy branches thrusting forth where they would and feathering the houses and street with soft shadows, each tree was a rigid box of leaves set on its trunk, its shade a precise square on the grass.

"Well, well," said Gummy at last. "How very tidy. How very tidy, indeed."

"But what have they *done?*"

Gummy shrugged. "Looks like Blaze the Pruner got carried away with a pair of snippers in his hand." He pushed back his peaked hat and rubbed his forehead. "Muggles, I have a feeling that you and I are not going to fit very well into this orderly scheme of things. Perhaps it would be better if we just quietly left now instead of going into the village."

"Perhaps—" Muggles hesitated, stroking her orange cloak for comfort. "No. I want to *see* everything just once more. And then there are the things I left here—things we'll need."

"Right." Gummy cheerfully began to pull in the rest of the boats and tie them.

They walked up the Street Going to the River

toward the marketplace, but although they saw a few figures crossing the square in the distance, the village had a curiously deserted and subdued air about it.

"I wonder where everybody is," said Gummy. "You don't suppose the judges have come and they're having a Something for them?"

Muggles shook her head. "We would have seen their boat."

They were just passing the candlemaker's cottage when Spill himself stepped out upon his doorstone. He looked preoccupied, but when he saw Muggles and Gummy, his face first brightened, then dulled, as though someone had struck a tinderbox to one of his own candles and snuffed it out the next moment.

"Greetings," he said cautiously. "What news?"

Gummy doffed his hat.

"Why as to that,
There's nothing much,
Except that spring
Is here to touch!"

"Spring—" Spill looked around with an uneasy motion of his skinny neck. "Ah, yes, spring. There's hardly been time to notice, you see. And how is Mingy?"

"Gay as a cricket," said Muggles. "Sitting on a wicket," she added with a sidelong glance at Gummy.

Spill's face went glum. "Seems I owe him three gold pieces. Mingy always said it was the money box helping me out, but Bros.—he's the new money keeper—says that's impossible, so it looks as though I owe Mingy. Not that I've got the gold pieces to pay him with," he finished with a despondent air.

"Mingy doesn't need the gold, but—" Muggles stopped, transfixed, as an idea occurred to her.

"But what?"

"But I'll tell him you've found out what a good friend he has been to you," Muggles said slowly. "I'll tell him that if he is ever in trouble, he can count on you to help him."

"Yes, yes, you tell him that. Not that it's likely, of course." Spill's scrawny neck angled about. "But I must not keep you . . ."

"Oh, you're not keeping us," Gummy said. "We all seem to be going to the marketplace, so we can walk together."

"Well, I, now, I hardly know," said Spill, hanging back.

"Oh, come along!" cried Gummy, giving Spill

such a hearty slap on the shoulder that the frail candlemaker almost toppled over.

Spill came along, his legs moving jerkily, his head tucked down into his neck as far as it would go.

The marketplace was as clean and shining as a new gold piece. Each little cottage with its green door and scalloped roof glistened in the sun. Even the cobblestones looked polished.

"It's very pretty," Muggles said politely.

Gummy pushed back his peaked hat and scratched his head. "I'm not even sure which one used to be my house. It's a bit muddling, not to say fuddling."

"Oh, you get used to it, and it's very tidy, of course," Spill assured him. His voice was muffled in his effort not to expose his face to the sight of the several villagers who were glancing curiously in their direction.

Bun, the baker's wife, approached with her laden shopping basket, so intent on her footsteps that she didn't see them until Gummy swept off his peaked hat and made her a low bow. "Good morning," he said.

With a little startled scream, she stopped so abruptly that a small fish skipped out of the basket and slithered on the cobbles.

"Allow me," said Gummy. He scooped up the fish and presented it to Bun with another low bow.

But she only backed off from him, looking wildly about for help. Her eyes fell upon Spill, who was pretending to be all by himself. "You, Spill," she scolded, "have you nothing to do that you stand idly about when everybody else is at work? Or have you become so rich that you can afford to pay a fine to the Council of Periods?" She maneuvered neatly around Gummy's outstretched hand and hurried on, leaving him still holding the fish.

"I really, that is, I must . . ." mumbled Spill in desperation. "I have many things to do. I know you'll forgive me if . . ."

"Of course, of course," Gummy said. "I see how things are with you. Fines for idling, is it?" He took hold of Spill's unresisting hand and slapped the fish into it. "Pray don't linger another moment. Off with you, my good Spill."

They watched Spill walk on to Supplys with his head humbly bent and his green cloak flapping about his spare frame. He didn't look as though he could ever be of any help to anyone, Muggles thought. Still, you never knew.

"Fines for idling!" Gummy gave a low whistle. "Think of the gold pieces they might have had from *me!*"

"How quiet it is," Muggles said. "Look, there's not a soul in the square but us—not even a child!"

Their footsteps slapped loudly in the silence as they crossed the marketplace, past the mayor's house, past Fooley Hall . . .

Gummy suddenly stopped and cocked an ear. "Listen." From the open door of Fooley Hall came a stirring and a rustling and a murmuring. Curiously, they tiptoed over and looked in.

Half a hundred small Minnipin bodies squirmed on as many stools. Half a hundred worried brows were creased in intense concentration as half a hundred hands painfully traced out circles and squares and triangles on sheets of rolled birch bark. Geo. the Official Village Painter strolled about the room inspecting the grubby work. On the platform Wm. the Official Village Poet bided his time by impatiently patting his foot against the leg of his stool.

Then Geo. began collecting the paintings and Wm. jumped to his feet.

"Time for poems," he announced, and a soft wistful sigh whispered about the room. "Hush your noise, now, or you will all miss your tea again today. You will each write a poem for me on the subject of winning the Gammage Cup." He paused to frown fiercely upon the children. "Yesterday two of you used 'sword' in your poems on the subject of playtime. This is the last time I will remind you that there is no such word in the Minnipin language.

Nor are there any longer folk by the name of Walter the Earl, Curley Green, Mingy, Muggles, or Gummy. You are to forget that such ever existed in our beautiful little village. Anyone heard using any of those names will be required to write two extra poems and will miss his tea for a week. They are bad names, wicked names, for they are the names that—"

But Muggles and Gummy stole away from the door and heard no more.

14

Fat sounds, thin sounds,
Sounds that make you start;
Queer sounds, near sounds,
Sounds that chill the heart.

Approaching sounds, encroaching sounds,
Of someone stealing near,
Creeping sounds, weeping sounds,
That make you shake with fear.

—Gummy, *Scribbles*
(Collected Works)

Back at the knoll, Curley Green and Mingy and Walter the Earl had been working furiously from the moment the string of boats pulled away from the dock.

"Be a good thing to get that roof on the new house," said Mingy when they had walked back up the knoll. "Be a nice surprise for Muggles when they get back." His voice was gruff. There wouldn't be any rare treat for lunch today without Muggles, who made the most ordinary fare rich with her herbs and sauces, and while Mingy frequently complained about Gummy's chatter, the prospect of a whole day without it made the hours ahead seem long. "Besides," he added grumblingly, "this sleeping out under a tree is all very well for wood mice, but when I woke up this morning, a spider was spinning his web from my nose to my ear. Very annoying."

"Hmm, yes," Walter the Earl agreed absently. He had said almost nothing since the incident of the tapping sounds and the glowing sword yesterday. This morning when the others got up, they had found his comforter neatly folded and Walter the Earl gone. He reappeared, hurrying up the west side of the knoll, just before Muggles and Gummy set out, but where he had been he refused to tell. "Just looking around," he said, and got out his iron box to pore over the ancient parchments while he ate his breakfast.

He was hunched over them now, and as he read, he fingered his sword.

Curley Green motioned to Mingy, and they went into Gummy's house. "He's been to the mountain. I know because there is gray dust on his slippers," she said, beginning to snap roots for a fish chowder. "But he doesn't want to worry us until he finds out— Mingy, what do *you* think made the tapping sounds?"

Mingy took a handful of roots and began to break them up into the pot. "Don't know. Wouldn't guess. What I say is, do what has to be done and keep a sharp eye. Right now we need a roof."

As soon as the fish chowder was simmering over the fire, the three set off for the marshy grove of willows west of the knoll. Walter the Earl hesitated between his sword and ashplant, and finally chose to take the sword.

Birds sang and dipped and flashed their wings and soared again into the blue sky, and the willows trembled in the breeze. They found a bank carpeted with tiny blue woodflowers.

"Spring ting-a-ling, ting-a-ling spring," Mingy sang in a voice like walnut shells being scraped over a rock. He stopped abruptly and cleared his throat. "What nonsense," he growled. "Don't know what got into me."

But Curley Green picked up the tune, and Mingy found himself adding his cracked notes in spite of himself. Even Walter the Earl came out of his reverie enough to rumble along with them:

> "Bright sunshine,
> Blue flowers,
> Pink rainbows,
> Moisty showers.

"Spring ting-a-ling!
Ting-a-ling spring!"

They began to strip the tender young willow wands from the trees, but even with the knives they had brought with them, they found it a wearying, difficult task. The wands clung tenaciously to the mother trunks.

"There ought to be an easier way," Curley Green panted. "I've never seen willow more determined not to be made into a roof!"

"Let's try the sword," said Mingy.

Walter the Earl looked dubious. "I don't know . . ." He felt of the blade and then touched it gingerly against a small branch. The twig was instantly severed from the trunk!

"It's like magic!" Curley Green cried.

"Uncommonly sharp," Mingy admitted. "Have a care! You'll cut your finger off!"

But Walter the Earl ran his finger straight along the cutting edge. "It doesn't *feel* sharp. That has been worrying me. Look." He held up his finger. There was only a small indentation where it had pressed against the blade.

He laid the sword lightly against another branch. The twig snapped off with a crack.

"Then it must be the secret!" Curley Green pressed

her own finger against the blade, lightly at first, and then harder as nothing happened. "You see! It doesn't hurt *us*—only other things!"

They stared wonderingly at the weapon until Mingy suddenly stirred. "Let's hurt some more willow wands, then. I'm going to fetch two more of the swords!" And he set off on a run back to the knoll.

Excited by their discovery of the swords' secret power, the three outlaws set the blunt-sharp edges to work among the willows. The blades cut keenly through the fresh green shoots, and the pile of wands grew higher and higher. When their stomachs told them it was time for lunch, they bound the wands into bundles and packed them back to the knoll over their shoulders.

"About enough for one quarter of the roof," Mingy observed over the fish chowder. "Uncommonly good chowder, this. What's in it?"

"I haven't the least idea," Curley Green confessed. "Some kind of roots that Muggles collected before she went off this morning. She says that all she has to do is *look* at roots, and if her mouth waters, they're good to eat."

Walter the Earl said little or nothing, but he kept his sword near him and his eyes often in the direction of the Sunset Mountains, just visible through a break in the trees from their knoll. After lunch they all stretched out for forty winks, and then it was time to go back to the marsh.

They worked through the long dappled afternoon until even Mingy was satisfied that they had enough wands to make a good tight weatherproof roof for the new stone house.

"How still it has become!" Curley Green said, leaning on her sword, which she had stuck in the earth. "I suppose we've frightened the birds away with our noise. But just listen. There's not a sound anywhere."

Mingy looked up from where he was tying a bundle of wands and listened. There wasn't the faintest rustle to be heard. An unearthly silence blanketed the marsh. Walter the Earl stirred uneasily and lifted his sword.

Then they heard it, though afterward they never could agree as to exactly *what* they heard. Mingy said it was a *fat* sort of noise, Walter the Earl claimed that it was an *approaching* kind of thing, but Curley Green described it as just a soundlike sound.

At any rate, it was *something*, and they stood immobile in the now-silent marsh, with the slanting afternoon sun speckling the shade all around them in eerie patterns.

As they stared about them through the drooping willows, Walter the Earl felt his hand grow warm. He looked down . . .

Like the blackness of night giving way before the slate-gray dawn, the sword in his hand was changing, changing, changing before his transfixed eyes. And as it changed, it grew less heavy . . .

"Look," Walter the Earl said in a husky whisper, but Curley Green and Mingy were staring at their own swords. He watched the slate-gray become pearl-gray, and the haft in his grip felt lighter and lighter.

The sound came again, through the hanging willow fronds, but he scarcely heard it, his eyes fastened on the blade.

It began to glow, then to shimmer, until he could no longer clearly see the edges of the blade, but only a radiance brighter than the sun at noonday. The haft was feather-light. And then . . .

Along the length of the blade faint marks appeared, burned there with a magic older than Gammage.

At the same instant, the sound that was fat, or approaching, or merely soundlike, changed to a whimpering, a squeaking, a wheeking. For a moment longer the faint marks showed, and then they faded. And the shimmering, glimmering radiance began to dim. The wheeking grew fainter and fainter as the light dimmed out of the sword. It dulled to pearl-gray, to slate-gray, and finally it hung black and heavy in Walter the Earl's hand.

In the branches above, a returning bird gave a cautious chirp.

15

A net across the Little Trickle won't catch fish in the Watercress River.

—Muggles, *Maxims*

When Muggles and Gummy came away from the door of Fooley Hall, they walked quickly down the Small Road Going Nowhere toward the last house where Reedy and Crambo the Basketmaker lived. Occasionally a curtain fluttered in a house they passed, as though somebody had stepped quickly away from the window, but otherwise there wasn't a sound or a motion on the street.

"It doesn't look as though we'd get much help, does it?" Muggles suddenly asked.

"Help? For what? *We* don't need any help."

"We might," said Muggles, frowning down at the glitter-stones on her cloak.

Reedy's face was stiff with displeasure when she opened the door to their knock. "Oh, it's you."

"Delighted to hear you say it," said Gummy,

doffing his hat. "I was beginning to think we weren't us at all."

"I suppose you'll have to come in, now you're here." Reedy stood aside ungraciously.

Muggles and Gummy entered the cottage. Crambo's handiwork lined the walls and bobbed from the ceiling—baskets in the shape of fish and in the shape of boats; enormous hampers, and receptacles so tiny that only a child's thimble would fit into them. By the window sat Crambo, his deft fingers working pliant strands into yet another basket.

"I can't say I'm happy to see you," he said without raising his eyes, "but now that you're here, you may as well sit down."

Muggles and Gummy looked around helplessly. There seemed to be nothing to sit on. But Reedy lifted two large willow hampers off their hooks on the wall and placed them upside down by the table. "Chairs," she said. "Sit."

They sat down while Reedy went into the next room. Crambo ignored them completely. After trying two or three times to engage him in conversation and getting nothing but silence in reply, Gummy rustled paper and wax-writer from his pocket and lost himself in his scribbles.

Muggles sat watching for a while and then got

up determinedly and went into the other room where Reedy was stowing Muggles's belongings in a large hamper as fast as she could work.

"You're very kind—" Muggles began.

"I agree!" Reedy snapped.

"Reedy, I know you don't believe in the fires—"

"Then why talk about them?"

Muggles felt her temper fraying. "You used to at least *listen* to both sides of a story!"

Reedy rammed a clay pot into the hamper and then stood up straight. "It's no use your going on at me, Muggles. I haven't anything against you, but I can't afford to have anything *for* you. So why don't you go back to your wilds and let us alone?"

"Very well," Muggles said. There seemed to be no way to reach Reedy anymore. Suddenly she blurted it out. "Reedy, listen! Suppose that—that we should be in great danger!"

Reedy peered at her suspiciously.

"What kind of danger?"

"Just . . . danger."

Reedy stirred uneasily and for the first time looked Muggles directly in the eye. "What could *I* do about it?" she demanded.

Muggles drew a breath. "You could listen—the way you always used to when you weren't afraid of the Periods. That's all. Just listen. Everybody else seems to have become deaf."

Reedy gave her a long searching look. "I promise nothing," she said at last. "At least—" She went into the other room and returned with a loaf of bread and a pat of butter wrapped in leaves, which she laid on top of the other things in the hamper. "There you are," she said. "You can keep the hamper. It's an old one the wood mice have chewed."

And with that Muggles had to be content.

When Crambo discovered that his two guests were really leaving, he became almost cordial and walked to the door with them.

"I suppose this is the last we'll see of you," he mumbled. "So I'll wish you good luck."

"And if—" Reedy said suddenly, then stopped.

"If what?" asked Muggles.

"If you see any of the Periods, you might explain that you only came here to get your stuff," Reedy finished rapidly. But Muggles was sure that that was not what she had started to say.

Muggles and Gummy trudged up the Small Road Going Nowhere, the heavy hamper swinging between them. There were two or three green-cloaked figures visible in the marketplace, but by the time the two outlaws reached the cobblestones, the square was empty, and the only sound was a small murmuring from the meetinghouse where the children were learning their new lessons.

"It almost makes you feel sorry for the lamprey, doesn't it?" said Gummy. "Do you wish you hadn't come, Muggles?"

"Yes. No. I don't know. But I'll be glad to get back *home*."

"Hst," said Gummy. "Advance the standard. Lower the hoist. We've got company ahead."

Ltd. stood uncertainly on the doorstone of the mayor's house, waiting for them.

"Ahum . . . greetings."

"Greetings," they answered.

Ltd. patted his beard with nervous fingers. "A-hum . . . I thought I should like a few words with you, if you . . . if you can spare me a moment."

"Certainly," Gummy said, and added in an impudent whisper,

> "But a flapping tongue
> 'Tis best to bridle—
> They fine you here
> For being idle."

Ltd. flushed from the roots of his beard up to his hair. "What I wanted to talk to you about— Ahum . . . er, some hasty words have been spoken, and some hasty actions taken, and I can't help feeling that there have been, possibly, injustices—on both sides, mind you, on both sides. Now, what I have been thinking . . ."

He's going to do it, Muggles thought in a sudden panic. *He's going to ask us to come back. We can come back home and everything will be the way it used to be before . . . before Curley Green and I ate those pepmints together and*— She glanced at Gummy. There was a peculiar sort of smile curving his lips.

"It seems to me," Ltd. went on, and his glance dropped to Muggles's orange cloak, then away as though the sight pained him, "it seems to me that these misunderstandings can be straightened out. We give in a little and"—he chuckled nervously— "you give in a little. What I am trying to say, in short, is that—"

"You are inviting us to come back to the village?" asked Gummy quietly.

"Yes, yes. Not exactly inviting, for of course there would have to be *arrangements* with those who . . . with those— But I see no reason why this couldn't be done, and the five of you could come slipping back into your old places—after the judges have gone."

Muggles looked at him blankly. "*After* the judges have gone?"

"Yes, of course. You could hardly come back before, could you? The Gammage Cup, and all that. You see—"

Muggles compressed her lips in sudden anger. "Yes, I see! And when we came slipping back, or *sneaking* back, which is what you really mean, so that you could feel cozy with yourself for forgiving us, you would start feeling ashamed of us all over again, but it wouldn't matter—*once the judges have gone!* And I would go on being poor simple old Muggles as though I'd never been away." She paused to snatch a breath and hurried on before Ltd. could raise his astonished mouth from his beard. "Well, I'm not poor simple old Muggles any longer, and I'm never going to be poor simple old Muggles again. Sometimes I used to write out my name Mgls. with a period, just to see how it must feel to be somebody instead of nobody. But I don't have to do that now. On our knoll, nobody cares how I spell my name. It's just me, plain Muggles, they care about, and I wouldn't put a period after it if you gave me one in a special meeting! So that's how it is, and I know you meant it kindly, but no, thank you, I'm not coming back before *or after* the judges have gone!"

Gummy picked up his side of the hamper. "I don't believe I have a single thing to add," he said. "Let us up and away, my dear Muggles."

They left Ltd. staring after them in stunned silence.

Gummy went on chuckling long after they had left the village and were paddling up the Little Trickle.

> "The finest sight
> I'll ever see
> Is Muggles's temper
> On a spree.
> Whee!"

It was well past teatime when they paddled under the willow fronds and made fast the boat at the little dock.

"Hulloa, up there!" Gummy shouted. "We're home!" But there was no answering call. Gummy made a wry face. "We don't seem to inspire welcoming committees today, my good Muggles. Heigh-ho, we'll just have to make the best of it."

Muggles took hold of one side of the hamper and he the other, and they swung it onto the dock. "You don't suppose they've gone back to the mountain?" Muggles asked, with an anxious glance up the grassy slope.

"More likely they're fast asleep, having eaten our tea as well as theirs," Gummy grumbled.

But when they had struggled up the slope to the top of the knoll with the hamper, there was no sign of the others and no sign of tea. Muggles bustled about, stirring up the fire in Gummy's house, putting on the kettle, and mixing batter for pat-cakes, while Gummy rattled around like a pebble in a box. When Muggles almost ran him down for the third time in her scurryings, she stopped in exasperation.

"Whatever are you prowling around about?"

"Swords," said Gummy. "I didn't want to alarm you until I was sure, but they've taken three of the swords with them."

Batter dripped off Muggles's mixing spoon onto the clean stone floor as she stared at him.

"You're dripping," Gummy said mechanically.

Muggles looked from the spoon to the floor as though they had nothing to do with her. "Are you sure? About the swords?"

Gummy nodded. "Of course, they may be using them to cut willow wands. There's a heap of them already cut over by the new house, so maybe they're down at the marsh getting more. Think I'll just amble along that way and see . . ."

"Not without me," said Muggles. "And we'll take the other two swords with us." She suddenly became aware of the puddle of batter at her feet. "Oh my goodness, look at the mess I'm making. Why didn't you tell me?"

A few moments later they sallied forth, bearing the remaining two swords. A sword was an awkward article to carry, Muggles soon learned. It was too heavy to hold long in one hand and too awkward to carry in both. After trying it all ways, she settled for wielding it like a walking stick and hoped she wouldn't harm the point.

They had scarcely reached the bottom of the knoll on the western side when Gummy's keen ears picked up the sound of cautious footsteps through the trees. He stopped short, his outthrust arm warning Muggles to silence.

For long moments they stood, scarcely breathing, until Muggles, who had come to rest in the middle of a step with one foot still in the air, thought she couldn't hold that stance a second longer.

Then a voice near at hand unfroze them. It was Mingy's familiar grumbling tones.

"I suppose," he was saying, "it's too much to hope that Muggles is back to make pat-cakes for tea."

They appeared through the trees, Mingy and Curley Green and Walter the Earl, and on their backs were tremendous bundles of willow wands, three times as big as they. In their hands they carried swords from which their gaze never wavered as they trudged wearily along.

Only then did Muggles realize how frightened she had been. "Of course there are pat-cakes for tea," she called in a shaking voice. "We couldn't imagine what had . . ." But she was talking to thin air.

At the first sound of her voice, the three had chucked their bundles of willow wands and leaped behind trees.

"It's us!" Gummy shouted. "What's wrong with you?"

The three emerged from their shelters a little shamefacedly, but their swords were still at the ready.

"We'll tell you when we get home," said Walter the Earl. "Give us a hand with these bundles, will you?"

It was impossible to talk on the upgrade to the knoll. There wasn't enough breath left among the five of them to form one sentence. Arrived at the top, they piled the willow wands beside the new stone house and paused to gasp. Then— "There is something in this valley besides Minnipins," Walter the Earl announced quietly.

"But *how?*" demanded Muggles. They were sitting in the open, finishing their tea and keeping close watch on the five swords, which were dangling from the roof of the sleeping shelter. Gummy had recounted their adventures in the village, but those happenings seemed distant and unimportant in the face of this new and terrible event that the others told of.

"But how?" Muggles persisted. "How did they get into the valley? They couldn't come down the mountain—nobody could—and besides, everybody knows that the only way into the valley is through the Watercress tunnel when the river is dried up, which it isn't. They couldn't—it's not *balloons*, is it?"

Walter the Earl shook his head. "I think we heard them yesterday, though we didn't realize at the time what it meant."

And suddenly Muggles could hear in her mind as clearly as though they were back in the abandoned mine—*Tap*-tap-tap-tap. Like fingernails drumming on a table, or raindrops splattering on a stone. Or, and Muggles shivered, like pickaxes chipping away the rock in an old mine . . .

"But *why?*" she cried.

"Gold," said Mingy, and the word fell like a chill upon them.

"In the ancient scrolls," said Walter the Earl, "I read that gold was one of the great causes of battles. That's what the marauders took away when they swooped down on Minnipin villages. Everything made of gold. Perhaps that's why the mines were abandoned. Even in this safe, secure valley, Gammage must have felt that the possession of gold was an evil that brought greater evil upon the villages."

But if they—the outsiders—had eaten so far into the mountain, they must have been at it for months, perhaps even years! Muggles looked at the others in dismay. All this time, while life went calmly on in the valley, something had been nibbling away at their peace, working to destroy them even as they tended the watercress beds and fished the streams and sent the mayor to Watersplash and had their holidays and fussed over the colors of doors . . .

"Of course, we don't *know* they are enemies," said Gummy. "Maybe the swords light up when friends approach."

"You didn't hear the way they whimpered." Curley Green gave a shudder. "They were afraid, horribly afraid, weren't they, Mingy?"

"Every bit as afraid as me," Mingy agreed with emphasis.

They fell silent then, each occupied with his own forebodings. Muggles went into Gummy's house to brew more tea, and while she waited for the water to boil, she made herself think of practical things, such as mending the roof—the roof that had leaked on Gummy that night of the fires on the mountains and waked him up, else he never would have seen them. And if he hadn't seen them, Muggles thought, he wouldn't have gone pelting back to Slipper-on-the-Water, and the sound of his slippers on the cobblestones wouldn't have wakened her, and she wouldn't have gone to the museum the long way round and so met Curley Green, and . . .

The water suddenly came to a full boil. *And the fin and the tail of it*, Muggles concluded as she infused the sassafras leaves, *is that now I am here, I shall see that the roof is mended*. She carried the tea outside and poured it into the cups.

The sun had disappeared beyond the mountains, and long shadows were drooping over the knoll.

"At least," Muggles offered as consolation along with her strong tea, "at least, we seem to be protected by the swords. Remember how the tapping stopped in the old mine when the sword began to glow, and then this afternoon, the . . . the marauders ran away in fright. So—"

"Oh yes," said Walter the Earl softly. "*We* seem to be safe enough as long as we have the swords. But what about the rest of the valley?"

"Oh." Curley Green sat up straight. "They could get around us, couldn't they? By making a wide circle where the swords couldn't harm them."

Walter the Earl nodded. "So it rather looks as though it's up to us to do something about it, doesn't it?"

16

The only good mushroom
is a cooked mushroom.

—Muggles, *Maxims*

But they were so weary and so stunned over the day's happenings that, talk as they would, they could think of no effective way of stopping the invaders.

"And for all we know," said Curley Green, "they might even be some sort of wild animal. How can we know how to deal with them when we don't even know what they are?"

"Wild animals don't build fires on mountaintops, but the rest of what you say is true enough," said Walter the Earl, and he fell to brooding over the problem while the others went on talking around him.

When night fell, they took turns keeping watch over the knoll through the long dark hours, each guard brewing a pot of sassafras tea for the next to start off with. But nothing untoward happened beyond a little skirmish between Gummy and an owl that tried to stare him out of countenance until Gummy hooted back at it and frightened it away. Muggles's watch was the last, when the night was old and the moon already sunk over the Sunset Mountains. To keep herself awake, she brought bowls and spoons and ingredients out upon the grass and stirred up batter for a breakfast honey-cake.

As the first rays of the sun streaked into the valley, Mingy grumbled and sat up. For a moment he looked about him in a dazed way, and then, as he saw the other sleepers, a slow smile spread over his face, but when he noticed Muggles watching him, he replaced the smile with an embarrassed frown.

"Morning," he said gruffly. "Anything happen?"

Muggles held up the bowl. "Nothing but a honey-cake."

"Good." He swung round to look toward the mountain, which was almost obscured by the trees. "You frightened?"

"N-no," said Muggles. "I mean, yes."

"Don't be. Won't get you anywhere. I'll go bathe." And he loped off down to the Little Trickle.

After a hearty breakfast of the steaming honey-cake, eaten outside within easy reach of the swords, the outlaws held their council of war. Gummy and Curley Green were all for raising an alarm in the village. Muggles and Mingy were uncertain, but

Walter the Earl, who had slept with his stout ash-plant in his hand, now thumped it decisively on the ground.

"Facts!" he snapped at them. "We've got to have facts—good solid hard facts that they will have to listen to. And the fact of the matter at this moment is that we haven't the slightest idea what we are up against. We are only guessing that the Mushrooms, the Hairless Ones, have come again. We don't *know* this. We haven't *seen* anything. And if the swords frighten these . . . these things off each time, then we'll never catch a glimpse of them."

"That's all right with me," Curley Green murmured.

Walter the Earl silenced her with a stern glance. "Now, my plan is this. I shall go alone, without a sword, to the foot of the mountain, and there I shall hide myself on that big rock where we picklicked the other day, and wait for the Mushrooms to appear, for though we don't know for a fact that they come from inside the mountain, we can reason that this is so. Then, when I get some idea of what they're like and how many there are and what weapons they have, I shall come back to report. If we can't handle them ourselves, we can then send for help." He folded his arms and sat back.

"But what if you should be taken!" protested Curley Green. "It's too dangerous!"

"In the event that I should be captured, which is doubtful, I shall have left a message written on the rock, describing these creatures. It's the only way."

"He's right," Mingy declared. "Only, of course, it's not Walter the Earl who will go, but me. If it comes to fighting a battle, Walter the Earl is the only one who will know what to do. We can't spare him."

"You're both wrong," said Gummy. "I'm the one to go. I'm used to stretching out in the open for long hours because I'm such a lazy fellow. And I'll do scribbles in my head to pass the time. Besides, I know the way better than the rest of you. And if I'm captured, it will be no great loss." He jumped up and clapped his peaked hat on his head. "It's all settled then."

"Sit down," growled Mingy. "Nothing is settled at all."

So they huddled together again under the tree to decide who should go and what the rest should do. It looked as if it would never be settled until Curley Green pointed out that the sun was getting higher with every passing minute, and the Mushrooms probably weren't going to wait politely inside the mountain until the outlaws' minds were made up.

"Very well," said Walter the Earl. "Then we'll let Muggles decide. She's got the best head of the lot of us when it comes to good sense. Go ahead, Muggles."

"Me?" She looked around at the other outlaws, but they were all nodding their heads in agreement with Walter the Earl's words. "My goodness, I don't know—" she began, and then stopped because she realized that her mind had worked it all out for her while she listened to the wrangle.

"All right," she said. "We'll all have to do the jobs we're best at. Walter the Earl knows most about battles, and that's his job. Gummy is the fleetest and ablest with his tongue, so he must go to Slipper-on-the-Water for help if we need it. Curley Green and I will undertake to feed anybody who comes from the village, and help with the armor." She paused and looked at Mingy for a long moment. "I think, you know, that Mingy is the one to go to the rock. He won't lose his head, no matter what happens. If he *should* be captured, he will know how to take care of himself until—until— So Mingy will go alone to the mountain."

Mingy tried to look his most ferocious, but the corners of his mouth kept going up instead of down.

Walter the Earl nodded his head vigorously. "That was well thought out. Mingy will go. And do you remember that high place about halfway between here and the mountain? The rest of us can wait there. We'll take the swords, and if Mingy gets into any trouble, we'll be close enough to come to his rescue. Is it agreed?"

"It is agreed," they all said solemnly.

They looked at each other for the space of a minute, and then Gummy jumped up.

"So on with the battle—
We'll make their bones rattle!"

They were almost ready to set off when Curley Green snapped her fingers and ran back to Gummy's stone house. She emerged with an old cloak the color of sun-warmed sand, which she pressed upon Mingy. "Put this over you when you get there. It won't show up the way your green cloak will, and it has a hood to cover your head. You'll look just like part of the rock."

"As long as they don't step on me," grumbled Mingy. He threw the cloak over his shoulders. "Thanks."

They marched quietly along the bank of the Little Trickle until they came to the high place, another knoll like that on which they lived. Mingy watched the others climb to the top, their black swords held carefully before them, and then he waved once, and set off alone upstream.

Mingy was used to loneliness in the village, but this was different. This was the loneliest loneliness he had ever known. And yet, strangely, his heart was light. He hurried along beside the stream, keeping a sharp lookout all about him. As long as there were trees growing thickly to the edge of the water, he felt sheltered and safe, but soon they thinned out as the soil became rockier, and Mingy felt big on the landscape. The mountain towered above him—were there any of the Mushrooms on top to see his scurrying figure below them? He made sudden sharp dashes from tree to tree, until at last he came to the great rock where they had picklicked two days before. Beyond it there was no shelter in which to hide.

Except for the music of the waterfall, all was quiet as he began to climb to the top of the rock. There were few toeholds, and the going was slippery. Once he almost lost the little bundle of food he had tied to his belt, but he clutched it with one hand and hung on with the other, and at last scrambled onto the flat top, where he flopped down and panted for breath. Then he crawled forward to a shallow depression from which he could watch the face of the mountain by raising his head slightly, but be hidden from view except from the highest mine openings. Arranging the sand-colored cloak over him, he made himself as comfortable as is possible on a rock in the hot sun, and settled down to wait.

The knoll on which the other outlaws waited with their swords seemed far behind him, but, by stretching his neck around, he could see the top of it over the scrubby trees. He almost thought he could see four little figures, as well, but probably his eyes were only playing him tricks. He turned around to keep watch over the mine entrances.

As the sun rose higher, Mingy got hotter. After a while he skinned off his own green cloak from beneath the sand-colored one, and tucked it under him. Then he had a drink of cold cress tea from the brass bottle Muggles had given him, reflecting that in a few more hours it would be steaming-hot cress tea, and that was a comfort.

"I'll be nicely boiled myself, come to that," he told himself. "A tender morsel I'd make, too," and he chuckled grimly.

The morning passed as slowly as a turtle climbing out on a sunny bank. Mingy yawned and fidgeted, and blew his breath upward over his nose to cool it and then downward over his chin to cool *it*, and fanned his hand before his face, and mopped his forehead, and yawned some more. He concentrated on the sound of the waterfall and tried to pretend that he was standing under it, but the thought only aggravated his thirst, and he had another sip of the tea. An early gnat found him and sang its song first in one ear and then the other.

"Go away," said Mingy under his breath, and swatted at the pesky thing. But the gnat hummed merrily off to tickle his nose, while Mingy's ear smarted from the slap he had given it.

He was just beginning to believe that they had imagined the whole affair of the tapping and the sword glow, when he saw the first movement on the face of the mountain. A figure appeared in the mouth of the abandoned mine—the same one the outlaws had entered two days ago.

Mingy froze like a frog watching his dinner fly circle about his head.

The figure stole outside the tunnel and blinked into the sunlight. He motioned, and two others joined him, and then two more. Mingy stared at them, his fingers digging into the rock. They were taller than Minnipins by at least a head, and they wore tight brownish-white clothes that fitted like skin, so that their round bellies bulged fat as puff toads. Their heads were almost hairless, and mushroom-colored

like their suits, as though they lived their days in dank caves, and they had ears twice the size of Mingy's own. Each of them bore a long stick with a wicked metal point—what Walter the Earl had described as a spear.

Mingy shuddered and closed his eyes against the horrid creatures for a moment. These *were* the Mushrooms, then. There could be no doubt. When he looked again, the number of Mushroom people had doubled, and more and more were pouring out of the old mine. Mingy counted fifty, and still they swarmed silently onto the face of the mountain. But he had seen enough. Time to start back toward the knoll to report . . . First, though, he must leave a message as he had agreed, just in case . . . The piece of soft red wax-writer felt wet in his hands as he scrawled words on the rock—hasty, terse phrases describing what he had seen. After one last look, he added "200—and more coming," and then, every nerve in his body alert, he began to slide himself backward across his rock. But almost at once he stopped in dismay. At his first scraping movement he saw the Mushroom people jerk their hairless heads erect. Instantly, the flow from the mine's mouth stopped, and the two hundred or more Mushrooms stood stock-still, listening, listening.

Mingy lay dead-still, scarcely breathing. After long moments he dared to lift his head again. The Mushrooms were filing out of the tunnel once more, but now they were scattering about the face of the mountain, their spears ready in their hands, their heads swiveling from side to side, listening, always listening.

Mingy frowned. It was absurd to think that they could have heard him move on the rock—he was too far away from them, and besides, the waterfall made too much noise. And yet something had startled them just as he moved. He watched their ugly bodies gliding about the mountainside, and then he noticed something else. They were examining each of the old mine entrances, not the way ordinary folk would, by peering inside, but by cocking those big ears at the entrances. Mingy slid the wax-writer cautiously out of his pocket and added a few more words to his message on the rock. At least they couldn't hear him writing, he thought with satisfaction, thankful that he was using wax rather than charcoal.

Then he began to slither backward, an inch at a time. He thought that some of the Mushrooms looked more alert as soon as he moved, but most of them—there must now be three hundred prowling before his eyes—just went on searching. With infinite care, Mingy at last reached the edge of his rock and stretched out a foot to find the first toehold. If he could once get down on the ground, with the rock between him and the Mushrooms, he had no doubt that he could outrun them. Those people with the bloated brown bellies were not made for fast movement.

He would have made it but for a piece of ill luck. Just as his left foot found a crevice, and he began to ease himself over the edge, his sweaty hands slipped on the smooth surface. He clutched frantically at a knobby protuberance to save himself from falling. The little slapping noise he made was no louder than a fish's glubbing as it comes to the surface to swallow a fly, but instantly there was a savage cry from three hundred throats. And six hundred legs started moving in a queer, lumbering, but deathly silent lope toward him. Spears were raised, ready to strike. Mingy might outrun those legs, but he would never escape the spears. With a mutter of despair, he tried to pull himself up on the rock again, on the tiny chance that they would go on past, but his foot was caught fast in the crevice. He yanked and pulled, and tried to wriggle out of the slipper, but it was no use. He was stuck fast.

So he clung, half over the edge, while the Mushrooms swarmed around the rock. With the wax-writer he scrawled one last message:

Caught

17

Gummy had a fleeting foot,
It never did impede him,
And everywhere that Gummy went,
That foot was sure to lead him.

It led him to the mine one day
And landed him in danger;
For when your foot is very fleet,
Then trouble is no stranger.

—Gummy, *Scribbles*
(Collected Works)

Back on the second knoll it had been a long morning, too, though a more comfortable one than Mingy spent. The four outlaws could just see the top of Mingy's rock, and they stared until their eyes ached for the first sight of Mingy himself. Then, perhaps ten minutes after he had left them, Curley Green put her hand on Muggles's shoulder.

"He's there!" she breathed. "I can see a little wiggle where he's climbing over the edge."

Then the little wiggle became one with the color of the rock, and the four outlaws settled back with a sigh to watch and wait. The morning crept by as though time had got stuck.

"You don't think we dreamed all of it, do you?" asked Muggles at long last.

"I hope so," said Gummy. He stood up and then sat down again. "Do you see anything yet, Curley Green?"

She shook her head.

Walter the Earl ran his finger over the black blade of his sword. With an exclamation, he did it again. "The blade feels warm!"

Muggles and Gummy touched their swords, but Curley Green kept her eyes fastened on Mingy's rock and the face of the mountain beyond.

"The sun has warmed them, surely," said Gummy. "See, they are still black."

"The blade was cold to the touch a moment ago," said Walter the Earl. "Can you see anything, Curley Green?"

"N-no," she began. "Yes! There *is* something. It looks like ants swarming onto the mountainside!"

They all leaped up to stand beside her, but none of the others had eyes as sharp as hers.

"There must be hundreds!" she cried. "They keep pouring out of the mountain!"

Walter the Earl swung his sword up before him. Its blade gave forth no light, but—was it their imaginations, or was it just a little less black than before? "We advance!" decided Walter the Earl.

Before the words were out of his mouth, the four started to run down the hill. At the foot they plunged to the right and sped along the Little Trickle toward the Mountain. As the trees began to thin out, they could catch glimpses of Mingy's rock in the distance.

"The swords!" Muggles gasped. "They're turning!"

A sudden savage cry smote their ears a terrible blow. An instant before, Muggles had thought she could not take another step. But the dreadful noise sent her lurching onward. Her sword began to glimmer.

Then she saw them—the invaders! Swarms of them pouring around Mingy's rock. And Mingy himself, pinned like a sand fly at the top.

With a cry, Gummy sprang ahead of the others and went winging over the stony ground, his sword gleaming in the sunlight.

A new sound came from the *things*—a whimpering, wheeking cry that grew louder and louder as Gummy carried his now-glowing sword before him.

"Wheek! Wheek!" They began to disappear behind the rock. But a few stood their ground and hurled a shower of spears at the oncoming Gummy. He darted aside and rushed on, untouched.

"Wheek! Wheek! Wheek!" The rest of the creatures went loping around the big rock.

Muggles gave a gasp of relief. Mingy was safe. She could see him move . . .

But the last four invaders turned back. With savage hands they wrenched Mingy's foot from the crevice and tore him from the rock. Swinging him between them, they carried him off to the mountain.

Gummy pursued them up to the very mouth of the old mine and plunged inside. For a moment they could see the white-hot flash of his sword lighting up the tunnel, and then all was blackness.

"Come back!" Walter the Earl shouted, but his voice only bounced against the blank rock face of the mountain. He turned a face suddenly grown bleak to Muggles and Curley Green as they came breathlessly up to him. "Folly to go in," he said. "Even with the swords—" He stopped and stared at his own blade. It still flashed with a searing blue-white light, and shimmering there were letters of gold.

"Read it!" Curley Green gasped. "Quick, it's beginning to fade!"

Walter the Earl read:

"*Bright when the cause is right.*"

He slowly raised his eyes from the ancient script, which was already beginning to disappear, and stared fixedly into the mouth of the old mine. "I have half a mind to— No! Gummy will turn back when he sees it is of no use. And Mingy—" He drew a sharp breath.

Curley Green started back toward Mingy's rock. "I'll see if he left a message."

A few moments later she signaled them from the top of the rock. When they had clambered up to her, past the scrawled *Caught*, Curley Green was standing in the shallow depression where Mingy's green cloak still lay.

The three stared down at what Mingy had written on the face of the rock with his wax-writer.

Mushrooms! Fat bellies Tall Hairless Carry spears 200—and more They hear me moving Are listening Big ears Get army quick

There was a hail from the tunnel mouth. Gummy! He staggered out into the sunlight and slid to the ground with a groan.

When they reached him, he smiled up at them, but his face was white. Blood stained the shoulder of his yellow cloak.

"A nothing,
A scratch.
I only need
A little patch,"

he murmured, and fainted away.

18

Creeping, crawling,
Fat things sprawling.
Slithering, sliding,
Mushrooms gliding.
Sneaking, peeking,
Hairless Ones seeking.
Quivering, quaking,
Minnipins shaking.

—Gummy, *Scribbles*
(Collected Works)

They got water from the Little Trickle, and Muggles bound up Gummy's left shoulder with leaves from the nearest tree and her orange sash. When she had finished, she saw that his eyes were open again, and color had come back into his cheeks.

"You're lucky it was only a scratch," said Walter the Earl severely. "Running into the tunnel like that was folly."

Gummy blinked at him and smiled. "Ah, but you should have seen the way my sword flamed in the darkness." He gave a rueful look at the blood on his cloak. "Of course, I suppose they could hardly miss me in that shower of light. But the way they ran, how was I to know one would be brave enough to aim at me?"

"Did you see Mingy again?" asked Curley Green.

Gummy shook his head. "I saw nothing but the sparks from my sword. And the spear!" He sat up abruptly. "Where is it? I brought it out with me . . . Ah!" His hand closed on the long shaft lying beside him. "We'll have to build a museum to put it in, won't we?"

"Can you walk?" Muggles asked anxiously.

Gummy sprang to his feet and then clutched at Walter the Earl to hold himself steady. "I can walk, talk, stalk, balk, and palk. Palk—new word. Wonder what it means?" He swayed dizzily, forced himself upright once more. "What are you all waiting for, a poem?"

"Gummy had a little sword,
Its blade was black as night . . ."

"He's delirious," Curley Green whispered.

"Nonsense," said Gummy. "I am simply overjoyed at finding myself the center of attention among Minnipins rather than those creatures." He looked up at the sun riding high in the sky, and became very sober. "What do we do now—go to the village for help?" He appealed to Walter the Earl.

"That's right. As soon as you can travel."

"Then lead on." Gummy hefted the spear in his left hand, wincing at the pain in his shoulder.

On the far side of Mingy's rock they picked up the other spears that had been hurled at Gummy. They walked as fast as they could, with fearful backward glances until the trees blotted out the mountain face. At first Gummy stumbled along, but after refreshing himself with cold water from the stream several times, he declared that he was ready to journey to Slipper-on-the-Water as soon as he reached the boat.

Muggles shook her head worriedly and caught up with Walter the Earl, who was striding ahead.

"I don't think Gummy should go," she said. "He's not really himself."

"What do you mean? He seems all right. It was only a scratch."

"I know, but . . . there's something queer about the wound. I didn't want to alarm everybody, and I washed it off carefully . . . It was a kind of sticky red substance that wasn't blood, though it looked like blood. It must have been on the spear tip, you see."

With an exclamation, Walter the Earl examined the points of the spears he was carrying. "There *is* something on them!"

"Yes," said Muggles. "I am thinking it may be poison."

Walter the Earl strode along silently for a few minutes. At last he spoke. "I shall go, then. See here, Muggles, I'll be as fast as I can, but it may take some time arming the villagers. If I am not back here before morning with the army, will you be all right?"

"Of course," Muggles said stoutly. "We have the swords to protect us."

"But the spears! You must be wary of walking outside the house."

Muggles nodded. "We'll wear armor."

When they had wearily climbed the knoll, Gummy slid down by a tree and closed his eyes.

"In half a mo',
    I'll get up and go,"

he murmured. "But I feel slow." His eyelids fluttered open and then closed again, and his head fell back against the tree.

Curley Green hurried to minister to him with cold water, while Muggles flew into the house to find her pot of herb ointment. By the time she had dressed Gummy's wound again, Walter the Earl was just rounding the bend in the boat, paddling with the fast current.

They scarcely noticed that he had gone. Gummy's pulse beat quickly and then slowly. Burning with fever at one moment, he shook with chills the next. They got him wrapped into his comforter under the shelter and fed him steaming herb tea. After a while there was nothing more to do except keep watch over him. Curley Green tried to wash the blood out of the yellow cloak, but the stain stubbornly remained.

"It's not blood!" she cried, looking closely at the cloth. Muggles told her about the poisoned spear points. "I hope that most of it came off on the cloak. Then of course the wound isn't deep." She stared gravely into Curley Green's eyes. "I think he has a chance."

At teatime they debated about where to spend the night, and decided that Gummy's house was the safest place. But when they moved Gummy inside, he started up and cried out that he couldn't breathe. Try as they would, they could not quiet him, and his fever raged higher, so they finally took him out again and made up their beds in the unfinished stone house that was still open to the sky.

They suspended the swords from the doorway and the three windows. While Curley Green built up a small fire in one corner, Muggles hastened down to the Little Trickle to fetch willow leaves for poultices and a supply of fresh water. The pot of ointment was disappearing at an alarming rate, so she stripped some willow bark and set it to steeping over Curley Green's fire. Then they brought three suits of armor and the five shields from Gummy's house and laid them beside the beds.

"It doesn't look very comfortable," Curley Green said, eyeing the burnished metal. "But I suppose we'll be glad enough to put it on if the Mushrooms come."

Though it would be several hours before dark, there was a long night ahead of them to divide into two watches, so Curley Green rolled herself up in her bed to take the first sleep, while Muggles propped herself in the doorway under the sword, where she could keep an eye both on Gummy and on the knoll itself. As long as it was daylight, nobody could come upon them without being seen long before a spear could be loosed.

Muggles thought about Mingy in the mountain, and then she thought about Walter the Earl at Slipper-on-the-Water, and then Gummy stirred and she bathed his forehead and changed the dressing

on his shoulder. The wound was inflamed, but Muggles thought it looked no worse than before. She
steeped some fresh willow leaves in the bark mixture
already brewing and added herbs from her stock.
Then she salved a bit of the remaining ointment
gently into the wound, laid the poultice on it, and
bound it in place with a clean piece of cloth. Gummy
muttered something under his breath—it sounded
like "Muggles had a gentle hand"—and was quiet

again. Muggles went back to her doorway and sat down under the black sword.

When it was quite dark, she moved inside. The swords would give her warning before the Mushrooms got close to them. Curley Green slumbered peacefully on, and Gummy's breathing sounded fairly even. In a little while she would waken Curley Green, but she wasn't really sleepy yet. The stars were bright in the sky overhead, and a few puffs of white cloud floated by. It was a night full of peace . . .

A spear whistled through the doorway. Then a fierce cry rang out over the knoll. "Kin-deth! Kin-deth!"

Muggles staggered to her feet. But the swords! They had given no warning! Stunned, she saw through the doorway by the dim light of the stars the shadowy figures of the Mushrooms creeping over the knoll . . .

Then with a sudden wild cry Gummy flung himself from his bed . . .

19

It is easier to lure a fish than to
hit it over the head with a club.

—Muggles, *Maxims*

Walter the Earl was well on his way down the Little
Trickle before the feeling that he had forgotten
something caught up with him. The spears! He should
have brought one of the spears with him to show the
mayor. But the current was sweeping him strongly
downstream, and to go back now would waste precious time. No matter, Ltd. would see spears enough
and plenty to spare as soon as he had rallied the
villagers to march against the Sunset Mountains.

He bent his back to the paddle. For years, ever
since he was a child and first began to decipher the
ancient documents that had come down to him through
his family, he had tried in vain to present facts to
the village of Slipper-on-the-Water. Here, at last,
was a fact that nobody could ignore.

Two hours later he was striding up the Street

Going to the River. The few villagers he met got very brief nods. Unconscious of their bulging eyes, he pounded on the door of the mayor's house with the knob of his ashplant.

When Ave., the Mayor's wife, opened to him, "I have come to see the mayor," he announced, and marched straight past her. Flinging open the door of Ltd.'s office, he confronted Ltd. himself and Co. the Town Clerk as they sat over a table covered with papers.

"Invaders have come through the Sunset Mountains!" he thundered.

He was greeted by complete silence.

"They have captured Mingy, and Gummy lies wounded by their poisoned spears!" Now there were slack-jawed stares. Co. half rose and fell back again. Walter the Earl thumped his ashplant on the floor. "Do you understand what this means?" he demanded. "Unless they are stopped at once, they'll have us all. Every Minnipin in the valley! We must raise an army! Now! Tonight!" Again he thumped the ashplant on the floor. "I have swords and armor for a band of fifty. In four hours of fast marching we can reach the mountains. The swords—"

"He has gone out of his head!" Co. choked.

"Don't be a fool, Co. There's not time for it!"

Walter the Earl turned to Ltd. "We'll send the food and supplies by boat—"

"These invaders," Ltd. interjected smoothly, caressing his beard. "Have you seen them, Walter the Earl?"

"Of course I've seen them! They've captured Mingy!"

"Ah. Suppose you tell us about them. What do they look like?"

Walter the Earl gave an impatient twitch of his staff. "Like Mushrooms! Great fat bellies and hideous bald heads—"

Co. leaped to his feet, his paunch quivering and his bald patch scarlet. "Get out of here!" he yelled. "Get out, or by Snowdrift and Frostbite, I shall tie your offensive tongue to your long nose!"

"Offensive?" Walter the Earl stood his ground against the advancing town clerk, raising his ashplant to defend himself.

"You see that, Ltd.!" Co. cried. "He is threatening me with his stick! He has gone mad!"

Ltd. seized his cousin's cloak and gave it a jerk. "I think," he said judicially, nodding to Walter the Earl, "I think perhaps you had better explain yourself."

"That's what I've been trying to do!" Walter the Earl smote the floor with the ashplant again.

"The invaders are the Mushrooms—the Hairless Ones—"

"No, no," cautioned Ltd. "Let's have no more fun made of poor Co.'s head."

"*I am not*"—Walter the Earl suddenly realized that he was shouting, and abruptly lowered his voice—"making fun of Co.'s head! I am talking about the invaders—"

"Yes, yes, of course," Ltd. said soothingly. "The invaders who have come over the mountains."

"Not *over*. *Through*."

"I see." Ltd. gave his beard a nervous jerk, but his voice still flowed like syrup. "Of course. So they came through the mountain. And what then?"

The terrible realization was borne in upon Walter the Earl that Ltd. was humoring him.

"You've got to understand," he said desperately. "This is no trick, I swear it. You would believe me if you could see Gummy. The spear had poison smeared on it—"

"Ah, yes, this . . . er . . . spear. Perhaps you brought this . . . er . . . spear with you to show us?"

"He did—in his imagination." Co. sneered.

"I left in such a hurry that I forgot it," Walter the Earl said dully. "Ltd.—" He fixed his eyes steadily on the old mayor's face. "Ltd., let me talk to you privately."

Ltd. wavered, but Co. cried out, "He'll do you harm, mark me! He's only come back to get his revenge. I won't stir from your side!"

There had been a faint flicker of interest in Ltd.'s eyes, but at Co.'s warning it died away. "Be quiet, Co. Now, Walter the Earl, we are your friends here, and we'll hear you out. Co. is a bit hasty with his tongue, but he will be silent while you tell your story, won't you, Co.? Good. Now then, you were saying that these invaders came over, that is to say, *through* the mountain . . ."

Walter the Earl stared at the mayor and Co. for a long minute. The mayor's face was kindly and sympathetic, Co.'s sneering; both were completely disbelieving. He turned on his heel and walked out of the room, past Ave. cowering in the hall, and on out of the house.

Standing in the middle of the marketplace, he was surprised to find that the sun had declined only a little since he had been admitted to the mayor's house—it had seemed to him that he was pleading with Ltd. and Co. for hours. Now he must think of something else. He must find somebody who would listen to him, somebody with sense, somebody who was unafraid to face a fact. Despairingly he looked about him at the few green-clad figures hurrying across the square. Thatch the Roofer? Thatch might listen, undoubtedly he would listen while he rolled his garlic about with his tongue, and probably even believe the story, but what then? Would he ever be able to communicate with the rest of the villagers with his "Well . . ." and "Well now . . ."? No, Thatch wasn't his Minnipin. Fin Longtooth? Too old and doddering to take fire at a new idea. Dingle the Miller? Walter the Earl's eyes lit up. Dingle was also the village songmaster and got folk to sing even when they didn't feel like singing. Perhaps—

With three long strides he caught up with Dingle, who was packing a tremendous sack of flour over his shoulder on his way to Loaf the Baker's house.

"My good Dingle, may I have a word with you? It is of the utmost importance!"

Dingle's eyes rolled behind white-powdered eyelashes. "Then you can't want to talk to me, Walter the Earl. I am of no importance whatever, save to mill and to sing. You must go to Ltd. the Mayor for matters of importance." He nodded toward the mayor's house and scarcely having broken his stride, continued on his way with all speed, but Walter the Earl doggedly kept pace.

"I *have* seen the mayor, but he won't believe me, and it's a matter of life and death to the whole valley!"

"I beg of you," panted Dingle, hurrying on, "not to insist upon following me like this. If the mayor won't believe you, how can you expect me, a simple miller and songmaster, to do so? The mayor is a Period, and very wise. What he does not believe, I cannot believe. Please do not make trouble for me, Walter the Earl. I am sorry for your plight, but I can do nothing." With a final spurt he reached the house of Loaf the Baker and disappeared inside.

For the first time in his life, Walter the Earl felt uncertain. All, all depended upon him. Even now, back at the knoll, Gummy's life might be ebbing away—the Mushrooms perhaps were sallying from the old mine to attack. And Mingy? He dared not think what was happening to Mingy. Fighting down a sudden panic that rose from the pit of his stomach, Walter the Earl forced himself to be calm and look about him. The marketplace was drowsily peaceful in the rays of the sinking sun. Occasionally a villager appeared, but one and all, when they saw him, ducked their heads into the collars of their cloaks and elaborately went another way.

Despair seized him—and then he saw Spill the Candlemaker. A dim memory of something Muggles had told about Spill prodded his mind—was it gold pieces? Gold pieces and Mingy!

Walter the Earl was beside Spill before the scrawny candlemaker could avoid him.

"Spill," he said hoarsely, "I've come for Mingy's three gold pieces."

Spill shrank away in terror from Walter the Earl's grasp. "But I don't have them! Muggles said . . ." At the memory of what Muggles had said, his face turned white, and he suddenly began to tremble. "Has something—has something—? Oh, please, I'm but a poor helpless old one and I—"

Walter the Earl cut his babbling short. "You're not too old and poor and helpless to rouse the village for him!"

"Rouse the—" Spill swallowed desperately.

"Listen to me! There's no time to lose!" Rapidly Walter the Earl sketched the events leading up to Mingy's capture, and every now and then gave the cringing Spill a shake for emphasis. When he had finished, Spill looked at him dumbly, but the light of belief was in his eyes.

"I need an army," Walter the Earl said. "I need every able-bodied villager capable of carrying a sword. I do not believe that the honor and courage of the ancient Minnipins are dead, but it is up to you to prove it. Rouse the village for me. Get everybody together at—" He frowned. Something more Muggles had said . . . Reedy! "—at Reedy's house. I'll join you there. Tell Reedy—"

Spill had slowly straightened his shoulders. For a moment, fire gleamed in his faded eyes. "You may rely on me." He gave Walter the Earl's hand a quick clasp and then set off with an awkward lope across the marketplace.

Thum, the miller's assistant, hurrying up the Small Road Going Nowhere, stopped short to gape at the sight of old Spill leaping along like a bird with a broken wing.

From some hidden depth of his lungs, Spill bawled at him: "I want every villager at Reedy's house! Spread the word! It's life or death! The invaders have come!"

Thum's eyes almost started from his head; then with a half-strangled cry, he darted to the nearest cottage, where he pounded on the door. "To Reedy's house!" he shouted. "The invaders have come! Sound the alarm!"

"Invaders! Spread the word!" Spill hammered on the next door with both fists. "They have carried off Mingy and wounded Gummy to near death!"

Doors opened all along the quiet Small Road Going Nowhere, and bewildered villagers poured forth.

"What . . . ?"

"What's happened?"

"Who is it . . . ?"

"Invaders! Invaders!" Thum bellowed. "To Reedy's house! Spread the word!" He turned and sped back toward the marketplace. "To Reedy's house! Sound the alarm!"

Spill went flying on down the Small Road Going Nowhere to alert Reedy.

And now the villagers took up the cry until Walter the Earl was almost deafened by the din. He didn't wait for more. Plunging into his old house, he tore at the trapdoor in the fireplace, half fell down the ladder into the vault. There wasn't time to put on the armor, but he took time anyway, his mind racing far ahead of his fingers. Then he flung one of the jeweled war-cloaks about his shoulders, snatched up a shield, a sword, and a trumpet, and clambered up the ladder into his house and out into the marketplace.

Thum was just racing back from the Road Pointing to Snowdrift. Behind him came a straggle of villagers making for Reedy's house. Thum gasped at the sight of Walter the Earl, veered in his direction.

"Here." Walter the Earl thrust the trumpet at him. "Blow on this to summon the rest and then come to Reedy's." He turned down the Small Road

Going Nowhere, but not before he had caught a glimpse of Ltd. and Co. in the middle of the square, helplessly trying to stem the overwhelming tide of villagers that poured past them.

Thum blew a shattering blast on the trumpet, then another and another as Walter the Earl threaded his way toward the last cottage on the road.

Villagers milled around Reedy's house, but they fell back before the glittering war-cloak and armor as Walter the Earl thrust his way to the door.

"There he is!" ran the excited buzz.

"The great warrior . . . ! Did you hear what Reedy said?"

"He's got one of the swords . . ."

"It turns brighter than the sun . . . That's what Reedy said!"

When she saw Walter the Earl, Reedy jumped down from the overturned basket she had been standing on, Spill and Crambo on either side.

"They're all ready to listen to you," she said quietly.

20

The best thing to do with a bad
smell is to get rid of it.

—Muggles, *Maxims*

Mingy came to his senses slowly. His head swimming, he started to pull himself upright, but a sharp
pain stabbed at his foot, and he let himself fall back
on the damp hard floor. A candle guttered over his
head, and a drop of hot wax fell on his forehead.
He stifled the groan that rose to his lips, but the hot
wax seemed to clear his foggy mind. He remembered
the hideous Hairless Ones dancing about him while
he was pinned to the rock, and then the glimpse of
Gummy racing toward him, his sword all but bursting into flame . . . But what happened then? He
remembered a sharp wrenching pain in his foot . . .
Yes, that was it. The Mushrooms had ripped him
from the rock and borne him helpless into the mountain.

They had thrown him down inside the doorway
of a cavernous room where candles cast a dim light

and there was an overpowering smell of damp mushroom. As the Hairless Ones gathered around him,
their puffy bellies jostling each other, he realized
that the smell came from them. They jabbered at
him and prodded him with their long clammy white
fingers. Then they began to argue among them-

selves, and the smell got stronger as they became more excited.

Mingy watched them dispassionately until it suddenly occurred to him that they were discussing what to do with their captive. One of them, whose stomach protruded farther than the rest, seemed to have the main voice in the argument. The others kept raising their spears against Mingy and chanting something like "Kin-deth! Kin-deth!" But the leader, he of the biggest belly, shook his head each time with an explosive "Nath!" As if to emphasize his feelings, he took hold of Mingy's hair and shook it until Mingy was afraid his head would snap off at the neck. But apparently one "Nath" from Biggest-Belly was worth more than a roomful of "Kin-deths," for the leader got his way. Mingy was shoved roughly against the wall and left alone.

The Mushrooms then squatted down about the cavern. There was a stir from the opposite end of the room, and an odor of hot rancid stew came wafting to Mingy's nose. Soon they were all gulping noisily and sucking their fingers.

Suddenly the leader gave an order. "Slurth en kath!" There was some grumbling, but Biggest-Belly repeated the order, and one of the Mushrooms brought a bowl of the repulsive stew to Mingy's side, delivering a kick in the leg for seasoning. Mingy turned away from the bowl, and the Mushroom, seeing that, snatched it up greedily and poured it down his own throat with great smackings and gurglings.

The pain in Mingy's foot had grown steadily worse, but nobody came to tend to him. At last he could feel the room going black before his eyes. He came to himself later—how much later he had no idea—to see the Mushrooms still in the cavern, but now they were dipping the wicked points of their spears into a pot of red sticky stuff. One of them carelessly swung his spear around after it was smeared red, and nicked another Mushroom. Immediately there was an outcry. Somebody fetched a metal pot from the corner near Mingy, hastily dipped a finger in, and painted the tiny scratch with a thick white substance.

Mingy noted that the pot was put back in the same corner after its use. Perhaps the white stuff would help his foot, if he could ever get to it. Mingy tried to pull himself up to look at the foot, but the pressure on it made him black out again.

This time, when he came to his senses, and the hot wax dripped on his forehead, he was alone in the cavern. The Hairless Ones were gone, and only the lingering dank mushroom smell remained to tell Mingy he hadn't been dreaming. Then he thought of the pot of white stuff. Cautiously he raised himself from the damp floor so that he could crawl. The pain in his foot made him stop every few yards, but he gritted his teeth and started out again after a few moments' rest. When he at last reached the metal pot, he lay beside it gasping for breath. Then came the agony of stripping off his woven slipper.

Muggles would do it so that it wouldn't hurt, he thought. But Muggles wasn't there. Muggles was safe at the knoll . . . He sat holding one thong of the slipper in his hand as the meaning of the spear-dipping struck him. What he had witnessed was an army getting ready for battle! In a frenzy Mingy tore at the slipper, unmindful of the agony. He stripped it off, and plunging his hand deep into the metal pot, brought out a great gob of the white substance which he plastered on his bruised and swollen foot. It was cool, with a soothing coolness that drew the pain magically out of his flesh. Mingy slumped against the wall with relief. He must make a plan.

Co.—how far away Co. seemed to be now!— Co. had once said that Mingy had a money-box mind. It was not meant as a compliment, but Mingy chose to think of it as one. Very well, he would now put his money-box mind to work. First, he must find something to eat, or he wouldn't be strong enough to act when the time came. That was easy. While crawling across the floor, he had been plagued by the packet of food tied to his belt. Quickly he opened it and began to munch on the bread and fish cakes Muggles had packed for him early that morning. The tea in the brass bottle tasted metallic, but it was strong and wet on his parched tongue.

Second, he must find the way out of the mountain. There were two entrances to the room, one at either end. Closing his eyes, Mingy called up a picture of his arrival in the cavern. He had been slung down like a bag of meal almost as soon as they entered. Therefore, the way back to the valley was through the nearer doorway. With satisfaction Mingy took another swallow of the strong tea.

Third, he must do something that would help the Minnipin army to destroy the invaders—always supposing that there *was* an army by this time. The Mushrooms must not be allowed to escape through the mountain, only to come back again and again. This was a more difficult problem and would take a great deal of pondering. It was idle to suppose that the Mushrooms had gone off leaving him completely unguarded. Anyway, whatever his job was, it did not consist of escaping. Somehow, he had to cut the Mushrooms off from the outside world.

Mingy extracted another fish cake from the packet and settled himself to a good, long, hard ponder . . .

21

The turtle whose head
Is within his shell
Thinks the world outside
Is going well.

—Gummy, *Scribbles*
(Collected Works)

Five reed-lights flared red and orange in the market-place of Slipper-on-the-Water, and the cobblestones resounded with the pat-pat of hurrying feet. From the west side of the square came the clink of armor as it was brought out of Walter the Earl's vault and piled in heaps under his family tree. Figures emerged from other cottages, burdened with blankets and pots of soup, hampers of food and cooking utensils, which they carried down to the dock to be loaded into the boats. In Fooley Hall the children were tearing sheets into strips for bandages. Over all drifted the aroma of freshly baked bread from Loaf's ovens.

His war-cloak flashing a thousand winking

fires, Walter the Earl hurried from one spot to another, directing operations, exhorting the villagers to greater speed. And while he strode the cobbles, he instructed Crambo, his appointed second-in-command, in the ancient art of warfare. But all the time he kept a careful eye on the small knot of Periods gathered round the center lamppost. Other Periods either stayed sullenly in their own houses or, like Wm. and Geo., wandered about making jeering remarks at the busy villagers. But so far these four—Ltd., Co., Bros., and Etc.—had done nothing but stand watch over the marketplace. It was unnerving, that silent gaze. Minnipins were giving the four Periods a wide berth as they passed.

When Reedy reported that the last of the food and other supplies had been delivered to the dock, Walter the Earl sent word to Fisher and his seven boatmen to finish loading the craft and embark at once. Then he signaled Thum to summon the villagers to the west side of the square.

Before the double blast of the trumpet had died away, Minnipins started streaming across the cobblestones. After a moment's hesitation, the four Periods at the lamppost, though holding themselves aloof from the throng, moved in the same direction.

Walter the Earl frowned uneasily and turned to Crambo, who was arming himself. "Get everybody lined up, and we'll pick our fifty at once. As soon as they are in armor, we'll march." He looked toward the mountains dimly outlined against the dark sky. "We'll go across the meadow to the Little Trickle and follow it to the knoll. Fast pace all the way."

Crambo, fastening his war cloak, was already bawling at the villagers to form a line. But suddenly reluctant, they hung back, their eyes fastened on something beyond Crambo and Walter the Earl. The four Periods had drawn themselves up in their own line facing the villagers, daring them to go farther.

"Never mind the line," Walter the Earl said. "We'll start right away." He walked swiftly past the small huddles, counting out his Army of Fifty. Eyes shifted, feet shuffled, but Crambo hauled out the chosen ones and sent them aside to array themselves in armor.

Walter the Earl hesitated before Geo. and Wm., who were on either side of Thatch, held there by the roofer's steel grip. Then he called out their names and Thatch's and started on.

"*Stop!*" Ltd. stood forth. "No Period goes on this fool's errand!"

Every Minnipin in the square froze. Walter the Earl stepped swiftly in front of the mayor.

"Periods are Minnipins like the rest of us. Give them armor, Crambo."

"I am still the mayor of this village, and I say that Geo. and Wm. stay here. I further must warn you that every Minnipin who goes on this night's journey will pay a fine before he is allowed to return!"

Crambo weighed first one foot and then the other, while all around him the villagers edged away from Ltd.'s angry beard. Walter the Earl cast a desperate look at his Army of Fifty, arrested in the very motions of donning their armor. He faced the mayor squarely.

"Geo. and Wm. go with us," he said. "They belong to the village, and the village has voted to go to the mountains—"

"Are you quite sure?" Co. asked with a sneer. He pointed to where the new warriors were standing beside the piles of armor. They were making no attempt to dress themselves, and some who had been in the act of strapping on the metal pieces began uncertainly to unstrap.

Ltd. raised his persuasive voice. "Good folk, return to your homes and your warm beds. You have only to look toward the mountains to see that all is peaceful there. The invaders exist only in Walter the Earl's mind, deranged by living apart from the village. Forget the alarms of this day. You were wrong to take action into your own hands, but we are ready to forgive—"

Walter the Earl half drew his sword. "Wait." Grimly he stared into the doubtful faces. "What you do in the next hour—in the next *minute*—means life or death to the whole Minnipin race."

Minnipins muttered and stirred and shifted in their places.

"Crambo," Walter the Earl said quietly, "go ahead with the arming."

Crambo nervously plucked at the fastening of his war-cloak. The Minnipins who had already turned away turned back to see what he would do. A waiting hush fell over the marketplace.

Then into the hush throbbed the sound—an unearthly deep-throated murmur borne on the night wind from the direction of the mountains.

For an instant there wasn't a flicker of movement in the square.

The sound came again—louder, deeper—and there was death in the cry.

"The invaders!" Walter the Earl pulled his sword. "Sound the trumpet! To arms!"

At Thum's blast, the square came furiously alive. Armor was snatched up. A dozen hands helped each warrior to array himself. Crambo counted out the

last of the fifty, and they scrambled into the remaining metal suits.

Walter the Earl turned to Ltd., whose face was suddenly drawn. "We need a medical band. Will you lead it?"

"I?" Ltd. looked around in bewilderment. "But I—"

"Yes or no!"

"Yes," Ltd. whispered.

Fifty jeweled war-cloaks winked in the fire of the torches as Walter the Earl took his place at the head of his army. Behind him Thum and Dingle the Miller held aloft the long trumpets from which floated battle flags of scarlet-and-gold. Crambo came running up to report that all was ready.

Walter the Earl thrust his sword into the air. "Sound the trumpets! Advance the host! Death to the invaders!"

"Death to the invaders!" came the answering roar.

The trumpets exploded with an earsplitting sound. With a fast marching step the Army of Fifty moved down the Small Road Going Nowhere . . .

22

When the magic in the sword
Burns its white-hot light,
Then the awful cry of "Kin-deth!"
Turns to shrieking, wheeking fright.

But when the magic flickers
And the light grows pale,
Then the fearful cry of "Kin-deth!"
Tears the night like hail.

—Gummy, *Scribbles*
(Collected Works)

When Gummy gave his sudden wild cry and flung himself from his bed, Muggles screamed, "Get back! You'll be hit!"

But Gummy leaped for the doorway and snatched the sword from its hanging. Instantly, it flamed into blue-white light that snapped and crackled until the night was as bright as day. But Gummy was fully exposed to the Mushrooms' deadly spears . . . With a cry, Muggles threw herself at him, and they went tumbling to the floor just as three spears winged harmlessly over the spot where he had been standing a moment before.

"Wheek! Wheek! Wheek!" cried the voices of the Mushrooms in the night, but they sounded close. "Wheek! Wheek!" The voices were moving around to the other side of the stone walls, away from the doorway.

"Help me!" Curley Green called faintly, struggling with her comforter.

Muggles left Gummy slumped in a corner out of harm's way, the dazzling sword still clutched in his fingers, and darted across to Curley Green. Two spears had landed, one on either side of her, pinning the comforter to the floor.

"Are you hurt?" cried Muggles, tugging at the embedded spears.

"No. What's happened? Never mind—"

"Kin-deth! Kin-deth!"

A spear hurtled through the window frame over their heads and hissed across the room through the doorway on the other side. Muggles ripped the comforter free with a shower of feathers.

"Quick!" she cried. "We must get the swords!" She sprang to the window to tear down the lifeless weapon. As her hand touched the hilt, the blade's sudden brilliant flare blinded her for a moment, and she staggered back just as another spear whanged past her head and landed with a stone-splintering crash against a wall.

"Wheek! Wheek! Wheek!"

"Armor!" gasped Curley Green. "We must put on armor!" She had pulled down the third sword, and was crouching under the back window, holding it aloft. The "wheeks" became fainter in that direction, but now they were circling around to the doorway again.

"Gummy!" Muggles shouted. "Wake up! Put your sword across the doorway!"

Gummy's eyes flickered open in his white face, and he stared at her as though he had never seen her before.

Muggles stamped her foot. "Gummy! You must wake up! Do you hear? Wake up! Put your sword across the doorsill!"

The faintest flutter of understanding crossed his face, and he smiled gently. With a tremendous effort, he pushed himself forward and then fell flat, the sword stretched out before him across the doorway like a line of fire.

"Keep your sword up, and I'll dress you," Muggles ordered Curley Green. She dragged two leg-pieces toward her and began the tortuous task.

"Kin-deth! Kin-deth!" Spears whizzed through the unprotected windows.

"Kin-deth! Kin-deth! Kin-deth!"

"They're coming closer," whispered Curley Green. "We'll have to think of something."

"Hold still," Muggles answered. "Here's your helmet." It slipped into place with a clang.

One of the spears angled through the window and rasped along the side of Curley Green's armored leg.

"Now!" cried Muggles. "Let's each take a side window and drive them off." She snatched up her sword from the floor, closed her eyes for an instant against the blinding light, and ran across the room, while Curley Green left the back window and darted to the opening opposite Muggles's.

The cries immediately grew fainter at the sides of the house, but louder at the back. Before any spears came through that window, Curley Green was there defending it. Muggles dropped her sword and began pulling and pushing herself into the second suit of armor. But before she was dressed, she had to snatch up the sword again and defend one of the side windows while Curley Green took the other.

"How long do you think it will take Walter the Earl to come?" asked Curley Green, breathing fast after two more dashes, between which Muggles managed to get into the rest of her armor.

"Don't count on him until morning," Muggles panted.

"We must think of something," said Curley Green. "We can't keep running back and forth between windows all night."

"You think while I do something about Gummy." Muggles turned to the still form stretched out on the floor. It would be hard to put armor on him, limp as he was, but he was in danger each time they had to leave the back window unguarded while they drove the Mushrooms away from the sides. A stray spear might find his body at any moment. The shields! She snatched up two of them and dragged them across the floor, but as she started to cover him, her eyes passed over that brave sword stretched across the doorway.

It was flickering . . . dying out . . .

"Gummy!" she choked, giving him a little shake. His face was white as birch bark. She put her hand on the hilt of the sword beside Gummy's relaxed grip. The blade flamed anew, but when she took her hand away, it faded again.

"Gummy! Oh, Gummy!" Heedless of the spears now coming through the side windows, she darted across the room to get the pot of ointment and the willow brew. Feverishly, she rolled Gummy onto his back, stripped the bandage and poultice from his shoulder, and slapped the remaining ointment in its place, with the willow leaves on top. But the sword still only flickered feebly.

"Wheek! Wheek!" The Mushrooms had worked around to the front again with the dying of the sword. Muggles laid her hand on the hilt and watched the flame leap into the blade until its golden letters shimmered. A last spear flashed through the doorway as the whimpering voices faded away from the front of the shelter. It sped across the room and clanged against Curley Green's helmet.

With an anguished cry Curley Green fell senseless to the floor. Her sword clattered into a corner, and slowly the light dimmed.

"Wheek! Wheek! Kin-deth! Kin-deth! *Kin-deth!*"

The voices were closing in.

23

One wood mouse can nibble
a large hole.

—Muggles, *Maxims*

Mingy was coming to the end of his pondering. The problem was, after all, very simple. Since he couldn't help raise the army or carry one of the swords against the Mushrooms, he would have to wage a one-Minnipin war of his own from inside the mountain. His job was to keep the Mushrooms from escaping through the old mine. He could only hope that the villagers of Slipper-on-the-Water were on their way.

Very well, then. He must use the materials at hand. He looked about the great cavernous room. Huge piles of woven mats were ranged along the side—sleeping mats? If the Mushrooms were pursued back to the old mine and found their way into the cavern blocked by those mats, what good would that do? Not much, Mingy decided. They would simply move the mats and come storming onward. A few more might be slain if the Minnipins followed them into the mine, but most of them would get through. Mingy let his eyes rove farther, but there was little more to be seen except for the candles guttering low in their holders on the walls. Candles . . . mats . . . Mingy scratched the tip of his nose and let a slow smile creep over his face.

Would the long passage leading upward to the open air act as a sort of chimney? He thought it would.

So—he'd better get up off his lazy haunches and set to work!

He wiggled his foot experimentally. It wiggled. Then he hoisted himself up and tried his weight on it. That was not so good. The white stuff had all worked in. He reached into the metal pot and helped himself to more of the healing salve. When he got out of here, that pot must go with him . . .

Hobbling over to the nearest stack of mats, he lifted two of them down. His nose wrinkled in disgust at the smell of the things. These Mushrooms would never work themselves to death washing. Pulling the mats behind him, he limped toward the entrance leading to the Land Between the Mountains and threw them down a few feet along the passage. Then he went back to the heap and got two more mats to add to the first two. He stopped to listen, but there was no sound anywhere under the mountain. If there were guards, they would be posted at the mine's entrance, and even their keen ears could not hear him so far away. Then he went back to the heap and got two more mats . . .

It was like the nursery tale Minnipin children wanted to hear over and over again: "And then *another* frog hopped down the bank and got *another* green buzz-fly . . ."

He said it over to himself with every trip across the floor. His foot began to pain him with each step he took, but he went on, back and forth, back and forth. And when the mouth of the tunnel was completely full, he still carried mats to stack alongside. There must be no lack of smoke for want of fuel, he chuckled to himself. But at last he couldn't manage another mat. He made a final trip to get his packet of food, almost empty now, the pot of white stuff, and two of the candles. Then he settled himself beside his stack of mats in the tunnel to wait and listen, and eat the rest of his bread and fish cakes.

24

The ringing clash as the bright swords slash
Goes pealing through the night . . .
And the Mushrooms' wail as they quake and quail
Brightens the swords' white light!

The song is loud of the warriors proud,
Who wield the swords that bite . . .
They seal the doom of the fleeing Mushroom
As they strike in a cause that's right!

—Gummy, *Scribbles*
(Collected Works)

Walter the Earl marched his men fast and faster
along the bank of the Little Trickle, but it was dark,
and unaccustomed as they were to any kind of walking except over familiar cobblestones in the daylight
they stumbled and fell behind and ran to catch up
and stumbled again.

"Light the torches," went the order back through
the straggling lines, and in a moment a dozen reed-
lights flared in the hands of the warriors. Then the

march was speeded up until Fin and Spill, with the medical band in the rear, could scarcely keep pace.

"Lean on me," Ltd. told Fin through clenched teeth, and Co. took Spill's arm to help him forward.

At the front of the line Walter the Earl kept his eyes alert for trouble. Was there a dim radiance there ahead of them, where the knoll should be? He felt his sword blade, but it remained cold under his touch.

Now Walter the Earl was sure that he could see a brightness through the trees, and he urged his men forward. They broke into a half trot, their jeweled cloaks swinging and glinting in the torch flares.

Beside Thatch, Wm. ran silently save for the sharp whistle of his breath through his teeth. The sound which had come borne on the wind from the direction of the mountains had badly shaken him. Now he was almost willing to believe Walter the Earl's story. He clutched tighter the ugly blackened sword that had been put into his hand, the sword that was supposed to flash with brilliant light upon the approach of the Mushrooms. Not that he put any faith in *that* part of the tale for an instant, but it was a comfort to hold on to something.

On the other side of Thatch, Geo. tripped over the sword which he had tied to his belt, and would have gone sprawling had not the powerful roofer reached out an arm to support him.

"Thanks," Geo. said in as cold a voice as he could muster from his gasping lungs. The near fall had jarred every bone in his body. How could anybody be expected to jog all night long lugging a bar of iron so heavy he wouldn't be able to lift it at the end of the journey! The sword caught him between the legs again, but this time he regained his balance without Thatch's clumsy help. That was enough! Here was one sword that was going no farther this night! Still trotting along, he managed to lag behind Thatch's bulk while he unfastened the sword from his belt. Then, holding it in readiness to pitch it into the next convenient patch of undergrowth, he accidentally touched the blade . . .

"Halt!" called Walter the Earl's voice from up ahead.

Geo. stumbled into the Minnipin ahead of him, but he scarcely noticed. The blade! The blade was warm in his hand and beginning to glow with an inner light! Awed, Geo. raised his eyes, and then a chill swept over him. Beyond the flaring torches of the Army of Fifty, high above them, the night sky glowed with light. Now that the army had stopped, he could hear a faint high wailing sound coupled with an even more ominous lower tone that chanted over and over, "Kin-deth! Kin-deth!"

Geo.'s faltering hand encountered Thatch's arm, and he clutched the strength of it, as though some of that power might flow into his own body.

Crambo came running back along the straggling lines. "Everybody forward for orders! Make haste!"

Alongside, the waiting boats had pulled in. Boatmen chucked out medical supplies and scrambled ashore to join Ltd.'s band.

Walter the Earl strode into the midst of his army.

"The Mushrooms are on the knoll," he said.

"Wheek! Wheek!" came the whine of the invaders mixed with savage cries of "Kin-deth!" The army stirred restlessly.

"We shall try to surround them, but there may not be time, for we don't know what desperate straits our people are in. Crambo and ten warriors will start to circle the base of the knoll immediately. They will take Dingle the Trumpeter with them. Then Brush and his ten will follow a few minutes later. Drug and his company go next. The rest will stay with me, including Thum the Trumpeter. I will give you as much time as I can to get into position around the knoll. Thum will blast the signal for attack. You will answer, Dingle, on your trumpet. No matter where you are, spread out and charge up the knoll.

Cut down the Mushrooms without mercy, but beware of their spears. Is all understood?"

"Yes!" they all answered in a hoarse, gasping shout.

"Good. Remember that we want to trap them on the knoll. If they run for the mountain, do not follow until I give the order. We must all fight together. Crambo?"

"We're ready!"

"Then off you go. Good speed!"

Crambo and his ten warriors and Dingle the Trumpeter melted into the darkness at the right, their single torch quickly lost within the trees. In two minutes' time Walter the Earl sent Brush the Cobble Sweeper on his way, and after a further wait Drug the Craftsman started with his company.

Walter the Earl kept his eyes fastened on the knoll. Though he couldn't actually see the houses on top from where he stood, the swords of the outlaws gave enough light to reveal flitting figures about the edge of the flat-topped hill. His eyes began to ache from the strain, but it was not yet time to give the signal for attack. Crambo must work his way around to the other side.

Then they all heard the anguished cry . . . The light from above dimmed . . . Instantly the high whine changed in key, was drowned by a hundred

throats chanting, "Kin-deth! *Kin-deth!*"

"Sound the trumpet!" Walter the Earl shouted.

Thum gave a mighty blast. The warriors surged forward up the knoll, Walter the Earl at their head. From the far side, Dingle's trumpet answered. There was a fierce battle cry from fifty Minnipin throats.

Armor clinked and rattled as the warriors raced up the hill. Torches were cast aside to sputter in the grass. Swords began to glimmer and then to glow. The shouts of "Kin-deth!" stuttered into startled silence, to be replaced with "Wheek! Wheek!" The

shadowy figures closing in on the stone house stopped
and turned in confusion. There was a whistle of
spears launched at the Minnipin host. Then the
Mushrooms began to run before the swords that were
bursting into flame all about the knoll. They were
heading for the roofless stone house.

But suddenly the dimming light from the stone
house flashed brilliant blue-white sparks, and Wal-

ter the Earl's heart leaped. A cluster of swords rose slowly above the roofless walls, showering fountains of light.

The Mushrooms fled in terror about the edges of the knoll, seeking a way out from the dread swords almost encircling them.

With a roar, Walter the Earl's men topped the rise. Spears rang against their shields and armor. There was a groan from one of the Minnipins, and he fell, a spear in his side where his armor was imperfectly fastened. On the other warriors rushed, leaving their companion to the care of Ltd., who, disregarding the flying weapons, knelt beside the stricken one to minister to him.

In a moment the whole hilltop was a circle of flaming swords, except for the side going down to the Little Trickle. Mushrooms fled toward the spot, but the swords pursued them, cutting and hacking and slashing. The night was alive with flame and shouts and shrieks and groans. Walter the Earl cut his way through three Mushrooms as he charged toward the roofless house, which was spouting blue-white fire. He burst through the doorway and stopped short.

Gummy lay to his right, his sword flickering feebly in his hand. Against the opposite wall, straining to hold the four swords high, Muggles teetered precariously on a mound built of shields, comforters, and—on top, between Muggles's feet—the limp form of Curley Green.

"They're still alive!" Muggles gasped, the swords wavering in her hands. "Curley Green . . . stunned . . . blow on the head . . . this was only way I could . . ."

Co. came running in. "They're cleared from the knoll!" he cried. "But they're running down to the Little Trickle. I'll take over here!"

With a nod, Walter the Earl was out the door. The last of the Mushrooms were pouring over the edge of the knoll down toward the stream below.

"After them!" he shouted. "Sound the trumpets!"

Ltd. came running up to report. "Five of our men wounded, none dead."

Spill popped up beside him. "Sixty-seven dead Mushrooms counted."

"Right," said Walter the Earl. Then the trumpets sounded, and he swung his sword in a flashing circle over his head. "Advance the host! Death to the invaders!"

"Death to the invaders!" came the ringing shout from all sides. The Minnipin warriors poured over the lip of the knoll after the fleeing Mushrooms.

25

Where there's fire, there's smoke.

—Muggles, *Maxims*

At first the valiant Army of Fifty seemed to be gaining on the Mushrooms, for their terrified whimpering sounded loud through the night, but gradually the "wheeks" grew fainter as the Hairless Ones drew ahead. The Minnipins had marched far, their armor hampered them, and even the swords, which had seemed almost to carry themselves flaming through the night, felt heavy in their hands. On before them, always out of reach, fled the Hairless Ones. An occasional spear still hissed through the air. Here and there a Minnipin went down, but his companions struggled on.

By the time Mingy's rock came in sight, the Minnipins were staggering and falling in exhaustion.

"Faster!" shouted Walter the Earl desperately. "Faster! Cut them down before they reach the mountain!"

The stumblers drove themselves onward at his call. But it was to no avail. When they pounded around Mingy's rock, they saw the Mushrooms disappearing into the old mine. Two guards at the entrance hurled spear after spear into the Minnipin host until the last of the Mushrooms were inside. Then the guards turned and were swallowed up with the rest.

"Halt!" Walter the Earl cried in despair.

The warriors fell in their tracks and lay groaning. The gold letters shimmered *"Bright if the cause is right"* for a few moments longer and then began to fade.

Ltd., at the head of his medical band, arrived and immediately began bustling about amid the weary army. But Walter the Earl strode tirelessly up and down before the entrance of the mine, sword in hand. Those nearest him turned away from the terrible look on his haggard face. In the east, the sky was beginning to lighten with the coming of day.

"Any sign of Mingy?" asked Ltd. of Geo., who was slumped against a big rock next to Thatch.

Geo. shook his head. "No sign at all. Likely he's . . ." But Geo. didn't finish the thought. "Walter the Earl wouldn't let anybody go in after him. Said we would all be picked off by spears."

"Walter the Earl is . . ." Ltd. began hesitantly. "That is to say, he has led the army well tonight."

Brush, who had flopped down close to the mine's entrance, suddenly lifted his head and sniffed. "I smell smoke!"

"It's coming from the tunnel!" yelled Dingle, pointing.

At first they could see only wisps floating out into the gray light of the dawn, and then the wisps became plumes that wreathed in the air and disappeared.

"Listen!" cried Crambo, and the clanking of armor ceased. Faintly to their ears came "Wheek! Wheek! Wheek!"

"They're coming back!" Walter the Earl shouted. "Stand out of the way of their spears! Crambo and Drug, your men on that side. Brush, over here with me. Ltd., take your folk beyond the big rock. Look to your swords!"

A ragged cheer went up. The blades were glowing brighter and brighter. Warriors scattered to left and right of the old mine entrance, which now belched great gouts of smoke, evil-smelling smoke that made the warriors cough when it blew among them.

"Phew," Crambo muttered. "These Mushrooms smell as bad as they look."

The "wheeks" came closer. Then, without warning, a shower of spears flew out of the mine, but they fell harmlessly between the two bodies of the army.

The first Mushrooms emerged choking from the mine.

"Cut them down!"

"Death to the invaders!"

Swords leaped and swirled and slashed like tongues of flame as the Minnipins closed in.

The slaughter was great that early dewy morning. When the sun rose over the Sunrise Mountains, plumes of smoke still drifted out of the old mine, but the work of the warriors was finished. Their swords were black now, and heavy in their hands. They went about the sober business of gathering the bodies of the dead Mushrooms into a great pile. Wood was brought for the funeral pyre, but Ltd. stayed the hands of those who would light it.

"Let us wait until we can go into the mountain to find Mingy," he said. "There may be more Mushrooms within to add to the pyre."

"Ltd. speaks wisely," said Walter the Earl. He watched the last wisps of smoke emerge from the mouth of the mine. "I want ten warriors to enter the mountain with me."

Every warrior stepped forward.

But just then they heard a cheerful voice singing—out of tune, it is true, but the words were clear. It was Gummy's Spring Song:

> "Bright sunshine,
> Blue flowers,
> Pink rainbows,
> Moisty showers.
>
> Spring ting-a-ling!
> Ting-a-ling spring!"

Mingy emerged from the mountain. His sand-colored cloak was askew, and he wore only one slipper, but his face was wreathed in a happy smile. Clasped in his arms was a big metal pot.

"Good morning!" he cried, "for I see it *is* morning. Is there anything for breakfast?"

26

Hail, all hail, to our outlaws bold!
They braved the forest and the mountains old,
And drove the Mushrooms from our fold
With their mighty swords of shimmering gold.
Oh hail, all hail, to our outlaws bold!

—Wm., *Scribble in Honor of
Five Heroes*

Messengers were sent back to the knoll and to Slipper-on-the-Water. With them went the metal pot of white salve which Mingy had brought out of the Mushrooms' cavern. But first Ltd. had smeared some of the precious substance on the warriors who had been wounded in the pursuit to the mountain.

Walter the Earl chose ten Minnipins to enter the old mine and search for more Mushrooms to add to the funeral pyre, but Mingy, though invited to lead the way, declined with thanks.

"You only have to follow your nose," he said. "As for me, it will be a long spell of famine before I ever eat another mushroom!"

Walter the Earl and his ten chosen men were inside the mountain all morning, and when they emerged at last, they carried three chests of gold ore which they had found in another cavern beyond the one Mingy had inhabited. They reported the entire length of the mine clear of Mushrooms.

"We rolled great stones into the entrance at the other end," Walter the Earl told Ltd. "Was that the right thing to do?"

Ltd. nodded his head. He hesitated and then asked, "What was it like—there on the other side of the mountain?"

"Gray," said Walter the Earl. "Gray and flat as far as the eye could see. No trees or grass or anything stirring. There was water trickling down the mountain, but it was sour and brackish. Not a pleasant Land Beyond the Mountains." He turned to look over the green valley now bathed in sunlight. "There may be other lands like ours somewhere in the world, but I shall never seek them."

"Nor I." Ltd. looked dreamily over the waving green trees of the Land Between the Mountains. "Tell me, what did your ancient scrolls say about Fooley's journey?"

Walter the Earl hesitated before answering, and then said slowly, "It was an accident. The balloon was made by a clever toymaker for a fun fair. But

Fooley got into it before it was tied fast, and when he threw out the sandbags, he went sailing over the mountains."

"I see," said Ltd. thoughtfully.

"How he got back is a mystery, except that the Minnipins of that time called it 'Fool's luck.' And he did bring back the things that are in the museum, and he did crash when he landed, but it wasn't the crash that addled his brain. He . . . was a very simple Minnipin, though a brave one."

"I see," said Ltd. again.

"I'm sorry," said Walter the Earl. "Nobody need know, of course."

"You are wrong. We Periods have been over-proud these many years, but we believe in justice—when we recognize it." Ltd. winced. "The painting and the family tree . . . were they really mixed?"

"Yes, but it doesn't matter," Walter the Earl assured him. "Before Fooley came back, there were no trees in villages because they made the place untidy with their falling leaves. So you see, it was a good thing after all. How could we do without our family trees?"

Crambo came running up to them. "The funeral pyre is lit, and the army is ready to march home."

But they only went as far as the knoll that afternoon. At Ltd.'s insistence, they rested there for the remainder of the day and that night. Ltd. sent off another messenger by boat, but nobody heard what the message was. Thanks to the white salve brought out of the cavern by Mingy, the wounded men were all better.

Mingy hobbled disconsolately about among the chattering warriors who had flung off their armor and were resting in the clean spring air. He didn't want to go back to Slipper-on-the-Water, that was the trouble. At least—he didn't want to go back to being alone again in his bare little house, with only a money box for company. Oh, of course, he had friends now, and Ltd. had talked at length about the sick fund while they were marching back from the mountain, but . . . He thought about the day he and Muggles had shared the turtle soup and fresh loaf in her cozy cottage. It had been a happy din-ner for him. If only Muggles felt the same way . . . He stopped short, frowning down at Thatch, who was stretched out against a tree, sucking blissfully on a clove of garlic. But how did he know that she didn't . . . ?

"I'll ask her!" he exclaimed.

"What?" asked Thatch.

"I said, 'I'll ask her!' " Mingy repeated. "Of course!"

Thatch watched him walking fast toward the roofless house and scratched his head. "Of course," he said. "Of course."

Inside the house, Gummy railed at Muggles and Curley Green and Walter the Earl.

"Can't you tell
I'm perfectly well?"

he grumbled.

" 'Twas the merest scratch,
Only needing a patch!"

"You don't get up until we say so," retorted Muggles. "You almost blinked out on us last night, and if Mingy hadn't discovered the white salve, you wouldn't be reciting your rhymes right now! So hush your noise!"

"A tyrant," Gummy complained. "A bossy, meddling tyrant you are, Muggles." He smiled fondly at her. "Not that I'm not grateful. If I had died, I'd always keep wondering how it all turned out."

"It's time for your hot broth," said Curley Green. "You can have a trout toasted for tea if you behave yourself." She still looked a little white, but the salve had healed the bump on her head where the spear had struck her helmet the night before.

Walter the Earl gave a stern nod of his head. "You do just what these two tell you, or I'll send you home by boat tomorrow instead of letting you march with the army."

Gummy returned to his grumbling, somewhat strained through mouthfuls of broth.

When Mingy poked his head around the door, Gummy waved him in with a spoon. "I'm making you a scribble, but it's not finished yet. It goes,

> "Down in the mountain
> Where the Mushrooms repose
> Lay Mingy the Fearless
> Holding his nose . . ."

Mingy scarcely heard him. "Look here, are we all going back to Slipper-on-the-Water?" As they stared at him blankly, he added in his old gruff way, "What I mean is, too bad after all the work we've done on this place. Wasteful. And then there's all that gold going to waste in the mountain. Ought to do something with it. Gold thread, gold cups, things like that . . ."

Walter the Earl frowned. "I've promised Ltd. to translate the ancient manuscripts for the village . . ."

"I don't know," Curley Green said hesitantly, looking at Gummy. "We've been talking about it. We thought perhaps it would be fun to live in both places. When we got restless in the village, we could come here for a week or two, or maybe for the summer . . ."

"Taking a wife
May lead to strife,"

Gummy interrupted with a grin.

"On the other hand,
It may be grand
And not so lonely
As on your only!"

"Oh." Mingy scowled. "Well, congratulations, I suppose. You don't want me around, cluttering up the knoll. If I had a wife now, and we fixed a roof on this place . . . Well . . . never mind . . ." He wheeled to go out, but at the doorway he paused and spoke over his shoulder. "Too cantankerous, myself. To get me a wife, I mean. Good thing, too, I shouldn't wonder. Married folk waste time—all the talking they do when . . ."

"Mingy—" Muggles's voice was so soft that he wouldn't have heard if he hadn't been waiting for her to speak.

He turned with his most ferocious scowl. "Well?" he snapped. "Speak up. Don't waste time. Got work to do."

"You haven't a thing to do," said Muggles stoutly. "And you'd better come back here and let me dress your foot properly. And so as not to waste your

cantankerous time, I'll tell you right out that if you want a wife, I'm it!"

Mingy leaned against the doorway, his cheeks glowing pink with happiness and relief. "Well," he said, "that's all settled then. Soon as my foot gets better, put a roof over our heads. Get it done next week, shouldn't wonder. No sense in wasting time. Suppose you'll want an orange door, or some such nonsense. Waste of paint, you ask me. But more waste of breath to argue about it." And he hobbled back into the room toward Muggles, a slow happy smile spreading over his face.

It was the middle of the next morning before Walter the Earl led his victorious Army of Fifty into the marketplace of Slipper-on-the-Water to the welcoming cheers of the women and children. Banners waved and the trumpets sounded. Garlands of spring flowers stretched from one end of the square to the other. The sun glinted on helmets and struck a thousand winking fires from the warriors' jeweled cloaks.

Another cheer welled up from every Minnipin throat, and another and another. The very cobblestones rang with the joyful sound.

"Hail to the heroes!"

"Welcome home!"

"Hail, Walter the Earl!"

"Hail, Muggles and Mingy!"

"Hail, Curley Green and Gummy!"

"Welcome home!"

Muggles clutched Mingy's hand in bewilderment. "Look," she whispered. "Look!"

But Mingy was already looking everywhere at once. The brave banners furling in the spring breeze bore names—the outlaws' names. Colored streamers of scarlet and orange and yellow and blue and gold fluttered from every house. And the doors! There wasn't a green door on the square. All—all glowed with rainbow hues.

"Pinch me," said Curley Green to Gummy, and then, as he obediently obliged her, "Ouch!"

Walter the Earl gave an order, and the army suddenly stopped being an army and became Minnipins home safe after the battle. Wives flew to embrace husbands, and children clambered joyfully over their fathers' armor until such a deafening clangor arose that it sounded like another battle. Then everybody embraced the outlaws and talked and laughed until the tears came, and talked and cried until they broke into laughter again.

In the midst of this scene, three strangers appeared from the Street Going to the River. Nobody noticed them at all, though they walked among the throng, listening to a phrase here, a sentence there, and exchanging glances as they slowly began to understand what had happened.

When the noise had subsided, Ltd. stepped up on a box in the middle of the marketplace. Dingle and Thum, seeing what he was about, gave three blasts on their trumpets, at which the strangers almost jumped out of their skins. The hubbub of the square stopped as though it had been choked off.

"Good people," said Ltd., "our brave army has returned victorious after slaying more than three hundred Mushrooms. We are proud of them. Some there were who could not fight because there was not enough armor or swords, but these tended the wounded and carried supplies and messages. We are just as proud of them. But there were five of our number who, after being wrongfully treated by some of us and driven out of the village—for they *were* driven out in spite of the fact that they outlawed themselves to save our faces—ahum, where was I? Yes, these five, though they had no reason to love their village, saved us from certain destruction! We are proudest of all of these five!"

A mighty cheer swelled from the throng.

Ltd. raised his hand. "Good people, when I say 'some of us,' I am referring to myself and to the rest of those you call Periods—the descendants of Fooley the Magnificent." He gave a wry smile before going on. "I have only just learned that this '*great*' ancestor of ours was anything but magnificent. According to certain ancient scrolls which Walter the Earl at my request has consented to place in the museum, Fooley's voyage to the Land Beyond the Mountains was no more than a foolish prank. He didn't make the balloon—he only stole a ride in it at a fun fair."

There were shocked gasps of disbelief, but Ltd. silenced them with another wave of his hand.

"So you see that the mayor of your village, who has borne himself much too proudly, is really the descendant of a Fool, for *that* was his true name. Good folk, I thought to bring you the Gammage Cup, but instead I have ruined your chances of winning it. I am sorry. I can only make some small amends now by resigning my office as mayor of Slipper-on-the-Water."

In the stunned silence that greeted Ltd.'s stepping down from the box, Co.'s voice rang out.

"Ltd. makes himself too much to blame! It was I who tried to outlaw our good friends, not Ltd.!"

"And I!" cried Geo. and Wm. together.

"One moment!" thundered Walter the Earl. He sprang onto the box, his jeweled cloak flashing in the sun. "We have had differences in the past, but when danger threatened, we found that there was no difference in our hearts. Ltd. is a great and good mayor. He says he has lost us the Gammage Cup. And I say, 'What does it matter?' If we are happy in our own way in our own village, do we need the Gammage Cup?"

"*No!*" shouted the villagers.

"But I am not the one to talk to you," Walter the Earl went on. "I say, let us hear from one of our villagers, who always sees the plain sense of things. I say, let Muggles come forward and tell us what she thinks!"

Muggles gasped as a new cheer went up. "Me?" She looked round for help, but many hands were pushing her toward the box, and she found herself mounted there over the heads of the crowd without a word to say.

"Pretend you're just trying to drive us to work," Gummy whispered up to her. "Go on, Muggles, we're all your friends."

"Good friends—" Muggles faltered, and stuck there for a moment, until she caught Curley Green's smiling gaze. "Good friends, I once said we weren't all the same color inside, but I know now that I was wrong. At least, well— The night of the battle we were all the very same color—a sort of shimmering gold, like the ancient writing on the swords. Of course, that was a big important thing. We couldn't go on having shimmering insides every day or we would wear ourselves out. We're . . . we're like the swords, in a way. Sort of black and ugly-looking when we're just going along from day to day and making each other angry over little things. But we ought to remember that way deep inside us there is a little flickering glow, and . . . and . . ."

"Go on, Muggles," urged Mingy. "You're talking sense."

Muggles lifted a fold of her orange cloak and began pleating it nervously between her fingers. "About Fooley . . . I don't know, but it seems to me . . . well, he lived four hundred and forty years ago, and it makes no difference what we *thought* of him yesterday or what we *think* of him today. He was exactly what he was, and nobody could change him by thinking. So I don't see how it can work backwards, either. I mean, Ltd. is what he is, no matter what Fooley was like. It's not Fooley we elected mayor anyway—it was Ltd. So that's all I have to say, except that I don't think we need the Gammage Cup. Our village is what it is, no matter what the three judges think of us, and for us it's the best village in the Land Between the Mountains. We don't need a Gammage Cup to tell us so!"

The villagers cheered wildly as she stepped down off the box. Thum and Dingle blew great triumphant fanfares on their trumpets. Banners waved and streamers fluttered.

"Hail, Muggles!"

"Here's to our village!"

"Hail, Ltd.! Our great mayor!"

Then somebody struck up a song:

> "Here's to our mayor,
> Good Ltd. the fair,
> Ltd. the wise,
> With far-seeing eyes,
> Oh, here's to Ltd. the rare!"

Hands were joined, and the singing, dancing villagers began to weave in and out about the market-place—round the museum, past Supplys, circling the mayor's house and Fooley Hall. At the head of the eel-parade, Fin the Oldest Inhabitant cavorted with all the vigor and joy of Little Co., who was next in line. Muggles found her hand in the friendly clasp of her neighbor Eng., and further along came Geo. and Curley Green, Wm. and Gummy. Walter the Earl and Mingy were drawn into the dance by Co. and Bros. Round and round went the villagers over the cobblestones, and then Fin led them out the Little Road Going Nowhere to dance in the green meadow beyond the village . . .

When the marketplace was empty, the three strangers looked at each other, and then looked down at the thing they carried, wrapped in purest reed-silk.

"This is the last of the villages we have to visit," said the first.

"There was no welcoming celebration for us like those in the other ten villages," said the second. "They never even saw us, so wrapped up were they in their affairs."

"They have had great trouble here," said the third.

The first nodded gravely. "But they are no longer troubled. Who knows what secrets were hidden from us by the other villages?"

The second rubbed his chin with a thoughtful forefinger. "They don't really need the Gammage Cup. You heard what the one called Muggles said."

The third took off his hat and then replaced it carefully. "But the terms of the contest say nothing about needing or not needing. It's all in the deserving."

They stood silent in the marketplace, looking about at the banners and streamers and garlands and the bright doors of the little white thatched cottages. From the meadow beyond came the joyful voices of the villagers in song after song.

"This village is what it is," remarked the first suddenly. "Nothing was hidden from us."

"It will be good to get back to Watersplash," said the second with a sigh.

"I am tired of gala dinners and speeches!" exclaimed the third. "Let us steal away quietly while the good folk are celebrating. We will never be missed."

They stayed a few minutes longer in the deserted but happy-looking marketplace, and then they hurried away down the Street Going to the River, their green cloaks billowing in the empty road.

But on the box in the center of the marketplace, glimmering and glowing in the afternoon sun so that the reflection of its light touched every cottage door, stood the Gammage Cup.

Carol Kendall was born in 1917 in Bucyrus, Ohio, and has lived much of her life there. In the fourth grade, she began her first novel. It wasn't very good and her teacher told her so. Despite that inauspicious start, Ms. Kendall continued writing, and when she was twenty-nine she published her first book, a mystery for adults featuring a twelve-year-old detective. After writing another adult mystery, she realized that what she really wanted to do was write for children. She went on to write more than a half dozen much-loved novels for young readers, including *The Gammage Cup*, a Newbery Honor book, and its sequel, *The Whisper of Glocken*. As she says of her preferred readers, "Children are a marvelous audience... they remember what they have read! Sometimes they remember it all their lives!"